In Bed with the Bachelor

In Bed with the Bachelor

A Bachelor Auction Novella

Megan Crane

In Bed with the Bachelor
Copyright © 2015 Megan Crane
Tule Publishing First Printing, March 2017

The Tule Publishing Group, LLC

ALL RIGHTS RESERVED

No part of this book may be used or reproduced in any manner whatsoever without written permission except in the case of brief quotations embodied in critical articles and reviews.

This is a work of fiction. Names, characters, places, and incidents are products of the author's imagination or are used fictitiously. Any resemblance to actual events, locales, organizations, or persons, living or dead, is entirely coincidental.

ISBN: 978-1-944925-33-8

Chapter One

J ESSE GREY WAS the most beautiful man Michaela Townsend had ever seen in real life.

So absurdly, dizzyingly, inarguably gorgeous that it didn't matter that he was scowling at her—that he'd *been* scowling pretty much nonstop since he'd slouched out onto the makeshift bachelor auction stage in the Montana saloon, in this pretty little town where Michaela's mom had grown up and where so many of her aunts and cousins still lived, supposedly to sell himself for a good cause.

She'd realized he was beautiful then, of course, through the din of the relatively polite applause of the assembled, primarily female, crowd who'd gathered for this event. It wasn't something anyone was likely to miss on that rangy, six-foot-and-then-some frame of his. All that mussed-up, dirty-blonde hair, as if he couldn't be bothered to tame it, so busy was he being growly and attractive, even in a situation like this charity auction where *some* of the other gentlemen had opted to spruce themselves up a little bit.

The better to kick start the bidding, no doubt.

But not Jesse Grey, who looked as if he'd just swanned in from moving heavy things with those sculpted arms of his, or had, perhaps, spent his afternoon riding motorcycles hither and yon like the epitome of some testosterone-fueled fantasy man. Then there were those delicious, milk chocolate, melt-in-your-mouth eyes to consider—not that *eyes* could melt in someone's *mouth*, Michaela chastised herself—and of course, that alarmingly fit *body* of his packed into jeans and a dark t-shirt, which she hadn't actually realized could exist in the real world.

That body, she clarified to herself, not the battered, vintage concert t-shirt he wore like a second, expertly distressed skin. It was all… washboard abs and the suggestion of those crazy diagonals dug over his hips and that masculine *hollow* between his pectoral muscles—

"I'm so sorry," Michaela said, blinking to clear her head, which was how she realized she'd been gaping at this man in the first place, there near the back wall of the bar in all the post-auction excitement. "I'm babbling. In my own head. I didn't actually know that was possible."

His scowl deepened. Improbably, it only made him sexier.

"I've never bought anybody before," Michaela said brightly. That mouth of his flattened, which seemed to have a direct relationship to that odd tugging sensation, low in her belly. She charged on, not sure what was spurring her along—that strange, new sensation, or the sense of something like panic that went along with it. "Not that I bought you tonight, of course—my family did that! I've never attended a bachelor auction in my life! Even for charity! Although, I don't know, maybe they're all for charity or they're just a Magic Mike strip club thing? My cousin Missy made it sound like she travels the world on a grand and rotating circuit of bachelor auctions wherever they might pop up, but maybe she meant she goes to Chippendale's a lot? Anyway, it was all her idea. She and all my aunts and cousins and they only each gave a little but that's why it added up so fast and—"

"Hey," he said then. Really, it was more of an order. "Breathe."

His voice was flat. Casually certain, as if he was used to instant obedience. And yet still a rough kind of velvet as it slid over her, like a caress—

An engaged woman should not have such thoughts, Michaela reprimanded herself, and then was instantly annoyed she'd had such a dramatic, conservative thought in the first place. Because her fiancé Terrence would more than understand. Terrence and Michaela were rational, reasonable adults who had long ago agreed that monogamy was silly and possessiveness was unattractive, and Michaela hated that she kept finding these little corners of ugly, outdated ideas inside her own head.

It was because this was her own pseudo-bridal shower, she thought then, and so what if her cousin Missy had somehow commandeered the initial shower idea involving baked goods and her aunt's living room and turned it into a bachelor auction at a saloon? That didn't excuse the weird, old-fashioned things that kept popping up inside of her at the strangest moments. More and more often, the closer they got to the wedding, if she was honest. She shoved that aside.

"I'm sorry," she said again, trying to focus on Jesse Grey, supernaturally beautiful human, as if he was a mere mortal. Because he was. Of course he was, despite appearances. That was the point. "I've never been given a—uh—contractor? Local-boy-turned-tycoon? Whatever you are?—as a bridal shower gift before. I'm not sure about the appropriate way to handle this situation."

She was still staring, wasn't she? It was like the whole crowd around them had disappeared somehow into the chocolaty goodness of his gaze, more compelling than the most wicked, decadent dessert—

"I'm Michaela," she said, sticking her hand out, in some parody of a normal person. A normal person who really, really wanted dessert. "Michaela Townsend."

Jesse Grey, the most gorgeous man she'd ever seen outside of a Hollywood movie, shifted slightly, so he was no longer leaning there against the back wall of Grey's Saloon. He looked down at her proffered hand as if it was spiked and potentially poisonous, and that seemed to take a very long time. But then, at last, he took it.

Mistake! Everything inside Michaela screamed, and she would have been annoyed with herself for that, too, but she was too busy being caught up in what was happening between them.

His hand was warm. Slightly rough, as if he sandpapered his palms or perhaps actually worked with those hands of his, with the long fingers she was tempted to consider elegant despite their obvious strength. That tugging thing inside of her shifted. Became heat.

He scowled as if she'd given him an electric shock, but he didn't jerk his hand away the way she was tempted to do. The way she should have done, she realized, a long beat later, when she only stood there, gripping him as if he was a brilliant burst of light and some kind of savior, too.

He was the one to let go. Eventually.

"Jesse Grey," he introduced himself, a considering sort of gleam in his dark eyes that made that heat bloom. Spread. "But you probably got that from the auctioneer."

It was only to be expected, Michaela thought in a slight daze, that a man who looked the way he did should also *sound* the way he did. All dark, sinful things and that rough edge besides.

"Like the bar!" she said. Idiotically. "The one we're standing in right now."

"This is a saloon, Michaela," Jesse said in a voice that was not quite a drawl, but wasn't quite so surly, either.

She opted not to reflect on what her name sounded like, coming out of that mouth. Like a month of desserts, all of them too decadent to be believed.

"This is the Wild West. And if you look behind the

bar, you'll see an old man I vaguely resemble, also named Grey. It's the family curse."

Michaela pivoted obediently and blinked in the direction of the figures behind the bar. All good looking men in that rugged, Montana way, and none what she'd consider particularly old—but only one man was standing still, half in shadow, his arms folded over his chest while he glared out at the crowd as if they were *doing something* to him by drinking his liquor.

"The surliness is the curse?" she asked. "Or the family resemblance? Oh, or maybe the saloon is the curse? Though I guess all those things could be connected."

She regretted that the minute she said it. It took a moment or two to look back at Jesse, though she could *feel* the way he looked at her, as if he'd set that whole side of her body on fire. Obviously, she told herself, this was what men like him *did.* That was why normal people didn't have much to do with such creatures, with all that fire and brimstone and drama, to say nothing of the intent way he gazed at her, then.

The room fell away again. As if it had never existed. As if the pack of her relatives, stuffed into two gleeful booths on the other side of the saloon, was little more than a memory. As if he was the only thing in the whole of Montana and the great, wide world beyond it.

"So," he said, his voice even, in a way that made her insides feel shaken loose from their moorings. "You won me. Or more specifically, a date in Seattle. Let me know the dates that work for you and I'll fly you out. We'll have fun."

The way he said the word *fun* seemed to dance down the length of her spine like the obvious lie it was. Or maybe it was that his definition of fun wasn't quite the same as hers. His, she was quite certain, included all manner of dark and tangled and needy things she didn't know anything about. She could see that as easily as she could see that ridiculously beautiful face of his.

"Oh, well." She almost let out a horrible, inappropriate giggle, but somehow kept herself from it. She'd felt this way once as a little girl, when she'd come face-to-face with a coyote on a hiking trail in the hills of southern Oregon where she'd grown up. Her parents had gone on ahead, around the next curve in the switchbacked trail, and she'd been briefly and terrifyingly alone. Just like back then, it was as if everything inside of her stilled, yet went on high alert. As if this absurd specimen of beautiful male was as dangerous, as predatory, as a wild animal. But that was ridiculous. "I actually live in Seattle."

That considering gleam in his gaze became more intent. "Do you now."

Nervous, she thought. A little bit wildly. *He makes me nervous.* She cleared her throat and told herself that was absolutely the right word to describe the sensations dancing inside of her. She was *nervous,* nothing more.

"Yes, and in fact, I think that's why my aunts and cousins pitched in to buy you," she told him. With perhaps a bit too much *nervous* in her voice. "They know who you are, of course, because so many of them are from here, and they really thought it would be a great idea to spend some time with you."

"For five thousand dollars." His voice had gone flat again.

Cool. Though his silky chocolate eyes were anything but.

"You probably could have just asked, sweetheart. I wouldn't say I'm a nice man, necessarily, but I don't bite." He didn't smile. She wasn't sure he could, despite the hard gleam in his dark gaze that felt like acrobatics deep in her gut, like a wicked grin from a different man. "Much."

There was a loud, buzzing sound. It took Michaela a breathless moment, then another to realize it was a kind of white noise and it was filling up her head. Her body's defense mechanism against imagining this man and his... *bite*. She thought maybe she was coming down with something, suddenly. She was hot, then cold. She could hear Terrence's reproving voice in her head then, warning her for the nine millionth time that if she insisted on reading those filthy romances in what little spare time she ever had, her mind would turn to mush. She always agreed with him that she should stop, that she should read Worthy and Important Works That Would Expand Her Mind and Impress Others, and then she went ahead and downloaded more of the books she actually liked onto her e-reader anyway.

Jesse Grey made her feel... mushy. Like a really good romance novel, in fact. The kind that took her breath away and kept her up half the night, desperate to see how it ended.

But it was the thought of Terrence that finally penetrated the haze she'd been in since her cousin Missy had shoved her toward this man to "collect her prize."

"It's not for me," she assured Jesse. Or maybe herself. "It's for Terrence."

He eyed her. "Terrence?"

"My fiancé," she supplied. Helpfully, she thought.

His gaze then seemed to pry off the top of her head and rummage around inside, and Michaela would have had to have been half-dead or an idiot not to recognize the danger in that, something far more precarious than *nerves*—but she didn't do a thing. She didn't look away, step back, run from him the way she should have. It was as if she couldn't. As if her body was going to do exactly as it pleased, and what it pleased was to stand right there in front of this beautiful, lethal man and... wait.

"You in the habit of setting up your fiancé on dates with other men?" Jesse asked, and there was a different note in his voice. Lazy, maybe, with an edge. It colored his gaze, too, making his eyes seem shot through with whiskey—

Or maybe Michaela had had too many of those slushy drinks her cousin Missy had insisted upon ordering by the table-load earlier.

"Only when it might help him out," she said, feeling

something much too close to drunk. It was definitely the slushy stuff, she assured herself. Nothing else. Not that *focus* of his, turned on her like that, as if she was somehow as fascinating as he was. *Certainly not.* "Terrence has had a run of bad luck, you see. It could happen to anyone these days, with the economy being what it is."

"Is Terrence an economist?"

Michaela thought the question was on the dry and pointed side, which was only one of the many reasons she needed to ignore all the *stuff* going on inside of her. She pushed on.

"My aunts seem to think you might be able to point him in a better direction, since you're the construction guru of Seattle. Their words, not mine." She laughed nervously. Definitely, that was nerves. "Do you prefer 'tycoon?' Is that pejorative? I know successful men sometimes prefer to pretend they're not all that successful, for various privacy reasons. Terrence was involved in this kind of weird hotel situation but it fell apart about ten months ago and he—"

"Please tell me you're not talking about Terrence Polk," Jesse said, his voice back to flat and a different, assessing light in his chocolate liqueur gaze. A light that made her think yes, this lazy, dangerous, coyote of a man could indeed be the successful businessman her relatives seemed to think he was, despite all that natural beauty of his, which had made her doubt it.

"Oh, do you know him?" Michaela asked in a rush

of… something. Something she knew had to do with that cool, crisp knowledge in Jesse's eyes that she very much wanted to avoid examining any more closely. With every last particle of her being. Because maybe the truth was, despite what she'd told Terrence and herself a thousand times, she wasn't actually *that* mature after all. "We're getting married in June."

THIS DAY HAD started fairly uncomfortably on the couch in his uncle's back office right here in the saloon and was now bordering on some kind of practical joke, and Jesse Grey was not in the mood.

First, there was the fact he was in Marietta, Montana, the place his extended family considered its historic seat, since various booze-slinging Greys had been in the area since before the actual official founding of the town in the late 1800s. Jesse had missed the traditional Christmas with the extended Grey family this past December the way he'd been doing for three years now, ever since his own father had found it necessary to seduce Jesse's girlfriend, marry her, then impregnate her—with twins, no less, and maybe not precisely in that order.

Jesse had decided he didn't need to be in the same room with his father or his father's blushing bride ever again, and no matter that his much-married and more-divorced father claimed it was True Love for him this time. Jesse had steadfastly stuck to his Zero Contact position—

no matter how many whiny, accusatory voicemail messages his old man liked to leave on his phone, especially around the holidays when Jesse's pointed absence was likely to cause the very commentary his father most wanted to do without.

But missing the big Grey family Christmas meant he felt compelled to come out to visit his grandparents around Valentine's Day each year. Not because he was filled with the joy of the manufactured holiday or brimming with the need for bright, red cut-out hearts or any of that crap, but because a single man of his inarguable means was basically a walking target at this time of year back home in Seattle. Jesse liked to take a break from the voracious women who were forever trying to tie him down to more than one night, all of whom seemed to lose their collective minds every February.

Or he usually got to take this time as a break, anyway. This year, he'd come out a week early to spend more time with his grandparents, like a dutiful grandson. And his jackass uncle Jason had decided it would be entertaining to mess with him, and had not only signed Jesse up for this auction, but had flat-out *dared* him to go through with it.

A man could walk away from many things, as Jesse knew from personal experience. But a direct challenge was not one of them—not when the challenger in question was a family member who would, quite literally, gleefully throw it in his face for the rest of his goddamned life.

"Why can't I write a check to whatever charity this is

like a normal person?" Jesse had demanded when his Uncle Jason had sprung this on him. Today. After lunch. "Why do I have to channel Channing Tatum to support this thing?"

"One, because I think it's funny," Jason had retorted in his usual gruff way, the only hint he'd ever laughed about anything in his entire life in the faint creases around his eyes, but it was only the faintest hint. It could also have been the weather. "And two, because I think you're too goddamned comfortable writing your freaking checks." He'd only shrugged when Jesse had glared at him. "Maybe you need to see if your body can cash one of them, for a change."

Jesse hadn't known what the hell that meant. But he had known better than to push his uncle on that or any other topic. His own father, Billy Grey, was a punk at best. He owned a regional sporting goods chain based out of Billings, Montana, where he made enemies and cheated on his various wives and never, ever suffered any consequences for his actions. Jason, on the other hand, was Billy's older brother and he was definitely not a punk. He was the current owner of Grey's and the custodian of the family's Marietta legacy. Jason didn't play games, pull punches, or suffer fools.

In the comfort of his life as one of Seattle's young millionaires, though his wealth had nothing to do with the tech industry that ruled the city and everything to do with his own sweat and labor and desire not to be his father,

Jesse liked to think he was more like his uncle than not. But he doubted Jason would agree with that assessment.

This, of course, was how Jesse had found himself succumbing to the indignity of this evening, an auction to benefit a little kid he'd never met with medical issues he didn't know anything about. It was that or punk out in front of his uncle, which was what his father would have done and was therefore unacceptable.

So Jesse had stood on that so-called stage. He'd listened to the auctioneer discuss him as if he was little more than a glorified cow. He'd been half-asleep, busy pretending he wasn't actually there, until the bidding had climbed above a thousand dollars. When it had hit five thousand, he'd been astonished. Who the hell had that kind of money to throw around in a sleepy little place like this?

He'd had an unpleasant sort of jolt when he'd seen the woman who was steered in his direction when he exited the stage. He'd hardly noticed the loudmouthed one acting like her usher. He'd zeroed in on Michaela immediately, as if she was brighter than everyone else in the room, and Jesse didn't like that at all.

She was delicate and gorgeous in the kind of fresh-faced, approachable way that made every part of his body lock up tight and hard. She looked like the kind of girl who should have freckles, the kind that danced across her cheekbones and made her taste like some kind of sweet summer crumble, though she didn't. She wore her dark brown hair swept back in an easy, friendly sort of ponytail he doubted she understood made her prettiness that much more pointed and difficult to ignore, and a long-sleeved magenta t-shirt that looked like a micro wool over a pair of casual jeans and winter boots. As if she was wholly unaware of her effect on every man in the room, with that mouth and that sweet ass.

And it took all of three sentences out of her mouth for him to realize that she must have no idea what she looked like, that she definitely had no idea that those lips of hers could start a riot, and that it was very unlikely that she possessed the kind of hardened, licentious casualness that he preferred in his disposable women these days. Not this one.

She was *earnest*. And possibly nervous, which should not have charmed him. She was intriguing. He didn't have to ask her if she liked casual sex and anonymous encounters, because he could tell by that particular look in her bright, hazel eyes that she had little to no experience with either one. Just like he could tell from his body's over-the-top reaction to her that he'd like to introduce her to the joys of each, if she'd let him.

Jesse doubted very much she'd let him.

He hated that he even wanted her to let him.

She was a problem, was what she was, and he'd never been more relieved in his life to hear of an engagement than he had been to hear of hers.

Until she mentioned that egregious loser, Terrence Polk.

Terrence Polk who was, among many other unsavory things—like a self-proclaimed "money and ideas guy" who never had much in the way of either—renowned to be just about the biggest slut in the greater Seattle area. That some woman was dumb enough to marry him was surprising enough. But a woman like this? Who seemed... nice? Actually nice, like a real person instead of the kind of fake, grasping, plastic creature who would make sense with a dirtbag like Polk? That was just wrong.

Jesse opened his mouth to tell her that. But there was something about her posture that got to him. She stood with her spine too straight and her hands folded too tightly in front of her, the way awkward teenagers stood in front of intimidating authority figures. He didn't know why that snuck under his skin and made him... restless. But Jesse didn't want to upset her.

And he didn't have one damned clue why not, when ruining people's days was a major pastime of his. He did it all the time as the owner of his powerful little construction company and he didn't care whose feelings he hurt when he did.

But Michaela was different.

Jesse hated "different." He wanted absolutely no part of "different." He'd thought Angelique was different, which was why he'd brought her home with him for Christmas that year. And she'd sure proved him right, hadn't she? He wasn't doing "different" again. Ever.

"To clarify, you want me to meet your fiancé," he said

after a moment, because he had to say something, or his head might explode. Or something worse might happen, right here in Grey's Saloon in full view of at least three of his relatives. "For business purposes. You don't actually want me to go on a date with him."

"I'm sure Terrence would enjoy any date you might plan for him," she replied, and then she smiled as if she had no idea what a reckless smile like hers could do. It was more powerful than it should have been. It made Terrence Polk, that piece of shit, seem like a decent person instead of the epic loser Jesse personally knew him to be. It made Michaela hard to look at directly, and not in a bad way. Not in any kind of bad way. Worst of all, it shot through him like pure sugar and too much heat, and he scowled at her as if she'd done it *to* him, deliberately. "He's very romantic."

"Have you actually met him?"

"I've been dating him for two years and engaged to him for six months." She didn't *quite* roll her eyes. "But no. We've never actually met."

"You've been engaged to him for six months after the two years or during the two years?"

She laughed, but not like she thought it was all that funny. "Because those six months are what make the difference? That's what determines whether or not I know him, in your unsolicited opinion?"

"I," he heard himself say, harsh and rough, like a complete dick, "am not going to go on anything even remotely resembling a date with Terrence freaking Polk."

He expected her to flinch away from him. Cry, maybe. He probably deserved it.

But Michaela only eyed him. Not without wariness. But not as if she was about to wheel around and race for the door or the safety of the group she'd come in with, either.

"Really, you don't have to do anything," she said calmly. Too calmly for his peace of mind, in fact, and he opted not to analyze why that snuck beneath his skin and stuck there. "My aunts and cousins mean well, but they shouldn't have interfered. Terrence has a lot of plans and a lot of balls in the air. He always does and, sooner or later, they always work out. It's just a question of waiting to see which one works out first this time."

And this was not his business, Jesse thought, looking down at this woman who had *complicated* all but stamped on her forehead. It wasn't his business and she wasn't his problem and this was not the kind of thing he wanted in his life in any way, shape, or form. Hell, no. It meant nothing at all to Jesse that Terrence Polk had managed to snow this admittedly lovely stranger into overlooking his basic worthlessness as a human being. That was her mistake to make, and the fact her lips were a temptation made real was unfortunate, nothing more.

This had nothing to do with him. *She* had nothing to do with him.

"Have him look me up if that takes longer than expected," Jesse said, so gruffly he was practically a parody of his uncle. But he figured there were way worse things he could be—like too involved with any woman ever again, for any reason. He'd sworn that crap off right along with his ex and his father. He'd meant it then and he still did. "I'll let him buy me a cup of coffee."

Chapter Two

THE ONLY THING more disconcerting than Jesse Grey scowling at her in the shadows of a wild west saloon after a long, strange evening was Jesse Grey in her Aunt Cathy's front hall the following afternoon, looming there next to the framed needlework and dated, vaguely floral wallpaper, looking six times more dark and annoyed than he had the night before.

"Oh. Um. Hi," was Michaela's bold, incisive response to the sight of him. She'd walked in from the kitchen, expecting to see one of her cousins after she'd heard the door slam, and she'd stopped dead in her tracks when it had turned out to be Jesse, of all people, instead. She assured herself that was a perfectly reasonable response. It wasn't every day a man who looked like Jesse turned up, much less unshaven and dangerous-looking, wearing those damned jeans and a knit hat tugged low, with nothing but a fleece against the snow outside.

Terrence would agree that this was reasonable. Rational, even, given Jesse's astonishing good looks. It would be odd if she *didn't* have this reaction to him. So there was absolutely no reason at all that she should feel something a whole lot like guilt that she did.

"What are you doing?" She swallowed. "Here, I mean?"

He glared, apparently not finding any of her responses all that reasonable, and she ignored the little part of her, down deep inside, that agreed.

"Are you ready?"

"Ready?"

His jaw, already a masterwork of carved marble, turned even more stony as she watched. "To go."

Michaela blinked. She was aware, on some level, that she was still standing there half in and half out of her aunt's front hall, rooted to the floor, like maybe he wasn't the only thing made of marble. "Go? Go where?"

That scowl of Jesse's took on a life of his own. The fine, masculine lines of his rangy body all drew tight and the way he glared at her should have knocked her back a few steps. Instead, she could only gaze at him as she understood, for the first time in her life, the real meaning of the word *dumbfounded.*

"Did you get hit over the head?" he asked, gruffly. *More* gruffly. "And let me give you fair warning. If you repeat that question back to me, I can't promise I won't lose my shit."

Michaela opened her mouth, then shut it, and she could have sworn the gleam in his dark eyes that followed then was her reward. Or his grumpy, pissy, overtly male version of laughter. Or one of the many things about him she definitely, one hundred percent, should not allow herself to find attractive in any way.

Hi, honey, she'd chirped into Terrence's voicemail when she'd gotten back to the upstairs bedroom she'd shared with her mother last night. *Crazy night! Who knew a bridal shower could take such a strange turn? Ha ha ha—but do I have a story for you!*

Luckily, Terrence had yet to call her back, which was not uncommon. Michaela reminded herself that she thought it was deeply silly so many couples she knew got all uptight about things like returned phone calls. She congratulated herself on the fact that she and Terrence were so much more mature than that, that they'd transcended all the childish jealousy and insecurity that marked so many of the romantic relationships of their friends. Thank God for their reasonable, rational, completely un-dramatic way of handling things! She was grateful every day. But the fact Terrence had been unreachable since Michaela had left Seattle on Wednesday night meant the story that was Jesse Grey was still hers and only hers.

Which, she thought as she gazed up at Jesse in her aunt's front hall that felt smaller by the minute, felt a smidge too much like some kind of intimacy.

"I'm sorry," she said. It occurred to her that she'd apologized an awful lot to a man she hadn't known existed twenty-four hours ago. There was something about that, which struck her as unbalanced if not outright wrong, and she frowned, which probably shouldn't have felt *quite* so liberating. "But I can't figure out why you're here."

A man wearing a bright blue stocking hat had no business looking that sexy, Michaela thought as he glared back at her as if her frown was a direct challenge to his authority. Or that… edible.

She needed to get a hold of herself. It had been a long night, filled with disturbing dreams, most of them featuring Jesse Grey and his astonishing abdomen, despite the fact she'd only glimpsed it beneath last night's t-shirt, and Michaela was appalled at herself. Deeply, resoundingly appalled.

Not that she was feeling whatever she was feeling and working that out in her subconscious, because there was nothing *wrong* with that, per se. Of course there wasn't. Humans were resoundingly *human*, she and Terrence always agreed. They were always going to do *human things*, at the end of the day.

But she couldn't seem to control this—*herself*—at all. That had never happened to her before. She didn't have the slightest idea what to do with it.

Hi sweetie! she'd sing-songed into Terrence's voicemail this morning when she'd woken in what she wouldn't call a panic, because that suggested things she refused to think about and were likely the kind of silly, overwrought nonsense she and Terrence didn't believe in anyway. *What a crazy weekend! I can't wait to tell you all about it! You're going to laugh!*

But right at the moment Michaela did not feel at all like laughing. Not when Jesse Grey was taking over the whole of the front hall as if he was a black hole, light and air and energy collapsing into him and simmering there in the set of that mouth of his, the glitter in his milk chocolate gaze, neither of which—she told herself stoutly—affected her. At all.

"I'm your ride," he said, after a long pause that Michaela thought might have lasted several years.

She stiffened, while her head toppled off into the gutter. She was certain he could *hear* it. "I beg your pardon?"

Jesse smirked. "I'm your ride," he said again. "To Seattle."

When she only stared back at him, he sighed and then jerked his head toward the door behind him and, she supposed, the world outside it she'd completely forgotten about since she'd set eyes on him. Again.

"A big storm's about to hit," he grated out. "I'm driving west because I can't get stuck here and they're grounding planes at the Bozeman airport. Your aunt and my uncle decided you should come along, but you're more than welcome to stay here snowed in until later this week. Your call."

She should have some kind of response to that. Michaela knew she should. She should *say* something, nip that crazy suggestion in the bud, assuring this odd and unfriendly man she absolutely did not need him to drive her anywhere, much less some seven hundred miles west to Seattle.

But instead, she stared. Every vivid thing she'd dreamed about traipsed through her head, kicking up heat and making her face go red, and what little air was leftover in the space Jesse Grey didn't take up seemed to sizzle.

The fact was, she needed to get back to Seattle. Fast. Her boss Amos was one of her closest friends after all they'd been through and all these years they'd worked together, but he was incredibly demanding and still her boss all the same. And that was apart from all of her own duties and responsibilities that she'd put on hold to come here and play The Bride for her very traditional and Very Concerned family members, who didn't understand a single thing about her life. Not any part of her high stress job and certainly not her relationship with Terrence.

Michaela thought if a big snowstorm was coming, the absolute last thing she needed was to stay here in Marietta one second longer than necessary. She would have to fend off six or seven thousand more rounds of the *what do you do again* game. Which was irritating after almost a decade, but still much better than the pointed prodding about her upcoming wedding, which was, in turn, no more than thinly-veiled, intrusive questions about hers and Terrence's relationship.

And if this morning were anything to go by, her cousins and aunts would do nothing but talk about Jesse until he'd achieved mythic status in her head, colonizing everything. Which meant, as strange as it sounded even in her own mind, that among all the other reasons she needed to get home ASAP, the quickest way to be rid of Jesse Grey was to go with him.

"I'm not packed," she said, like the idiot she was in this man's presence and nowhere else.

And that marvelous mouth of his curved then, as something that might have been humor, if much harder, moved through his gaze.

"You have five minutes."

Michaela took more like twenty-five. She confirmed her flight out of Bozeman that evening really was likely to be cancelled, she texted Amos to inform him the weather might keep her away from the office longer than she'd planned and he should try not to freak out, and she threw her things into her small, carry-on roller bag. Then she paused to make the usual series of mild death threats to her meddling, irritating, cackling relatives, gathered around her aunt's kitchen table, until her mother cut her off midstream. Bonnie Townsend sipped at her coffee in that delicate way of hers that made Michaela feel like some kind of lumbering wildebeest in comparison, the perfectly-shaped eyebrows Michaela had been envious of all her life high on her forehead.

"My goodness, Michaela," she murmured in repressive tones. The same way she'd chastised Michaela for her impatience with her family's inability to understand every last one of her life choices only last night. *They want to know these things because they love you, not because they want to annoy you. I don't think it would hurt you to try to remember that.* "If you're not interested in having a favor done for you, I'm certain there are more gracious ways to say so."

Feeling suitably chastened and about an inch tall, as ever, Michaela buttoned her lip and wheeled her suitcase out into the hall, where Jesse Grey was making like a column of granite. Except less approachable and far less sunny of disposition.

"Okay!" she chirped like some kind of psychotic kindergarten teacher, as if that might soften him up. "I'm ready!"

He exuded grittiness without seeming to do anything but stand there, and she felt that tugging thing low in her belly again, even more insistent today than it had been the night before.

There was *human*, she thought then, and then there was straight up *destructive*, and she wasn't sure she could tell the difference. It had never been an issue before.

"Are you sure?" he asked in that low rumble of a voice. "Maybe you want to say goodbye to everyone down on Main Street, too? The outlying ranches? The whole of Montana while you're at it?"

"What's interesting about you, Jesse," she said, and it was a bit of a fight to keep hold of her not-entirely-polite smile, "is that you're possibly the most unfriendly man I've ever met. Why did anyone think you'd make a good bachelor auction item?"

"Must be you," he replied, with an almost-smile that didn't ease the bite of his words at all. "This is the friendliest I've been in years. To anyone."

"Childhood trauma?"

His mouth went lethal then. "Something like that."

"What fun," she said, and beamed at him like she meant it. "And we have hours upon hours trapped in a car together! Hooray!"

He moved then, which was something a little more than surprising, or at least that was how she interpreted that liquid thing that washed through her and that jolt that catapulted from her heart to her feet and back up again.

"Be nice," he growled. "Or I'll make you carry your own damned bag."

She couldn't breathe. Or process that.

"I always carry my own bag," she informed him, on autopilot. "I'm a liberated woman, thank you. My partner isn't a bellhop. What does that even mean?"

He muttered something that sounded filthy, which Michaela told herself was further evidence he was terrible in every way, but that wasn't what the swirling, heated thing inside her felt about any of this. Definitely not.

"It means your man is a douche," he growled at her.

He reached over and hefted up her heavy, rolling suitcase as if it weighed about as much as a feather pillow, then turned and stalked out of the house, leaving Michaela no choice but to follow after him.

The air outside was razor sharp and viciously cold, a far

cry from the softer wet of the Pacific Northwest winters Michaela had grown up with and even loved. She shuddered out a breath but kept going, following Jesse down her aunt's carefully shoveled front path and out to where one of those Range Rover-type half-jeep/half-truck vehicles sat at the curb, gleaming black and powerful and as irritating as its driver. Jesse threw her bag in the far back, slammed the door shut, and then jerked his head toward the passenger side.

"Let's go." It wasn't an invitation. It was an order. Another order. He clearly liked issuing them.

"Did you just call my—" She couldn't call Terrence her *man*. That made her sound... something. A possessive, jealous hoarder, to start. "Did you call Terrence a douche?"

Jesse managed to give the distinct impression of rolling his eyes skyward and sighing heavily without actually doing either of those things. He rounded the side of the SUV and opened the passenger door for her in a stark, annoyed manner that stripped the act of any possible chivalric content even as he did it.

"In the car," he said. "Now."

"Terrence is not a douche," Michaela said stoutly, crossing her arms over her chest and wishing she were wearing several more layers beneath her winter jacket as the Marietta wind slapped at her. "And even if he was, I'm engaged to him, so your default assumption should be that I'm into that. So why would you go out of your way to insult someone's fiancé?"

"Michaela."

He gritted out her name and there was nothing the least bit sweet or appealing about it. It was about the furthest thing from *nice* she'd ever heard. And yet for a moment her legs felt as if they might go out from under her, toppling her sideways into the nearest snow bank.

Ice, she told herself sagely. *Nothing but ice.*

Definitely not the sound of her name, all sandpaper and whiskey, sliding over her and abrading her skin as it went—

"Look up."

She did as he commanded because that was far preferable to policing her own distressingly wayward thoughts just then. She tipped her head back and looked up at the Montana sky, which was clouded over and swollen with portent.

"It's going to snow," Jesse said, very distinctly, as if he was beginning to suspect she was not very bright. She couldn't help but agree with that assessment. He made her feel like a fool. "Soon and at great length. You can either get in the goddamned truck and try to beat the storm with me, or you can sit here for however long it takes them to dig out. Your choice, but you need to make it now."

She felt like Little Red Riding Hood, peering at a set of sharp, gleaming fangs, telling herself it wasn't a wolf when she knew very well that he was. Of course he was. But her other alternative was more time away from work, which was always a headache, and more time with her family meant it would really be more like a migraine. Michaela loved her family. She did. But none of them seemed to understand that she was no longer thirteen and that she was, in fact, capable of making her own decisions. She was tired of explaining what she did for Amos, just as she was tired of defending Terrence to them. Jesse Grey might be a jerk, but he was the fastest way home to her actual life, where she was highly-valued in both her professional and private arenas and no one required her to defend anything.

Michaela got in the SUV and sat there questioning her life choices while he shut her door behind her, like some dangerous remnant of an old school gentleman. She told herself she found that infantilizing and offensive—but the warmth that twisted around in her belly suggested otherwise.

Something restless and worrying snaked through her, making her shiver, as Jesse loped around the front bumper, still scowling. She thought his face might actually be stuck that way—that it might in fact be medical. And she didn't understand why that failed to make him the slightest bit less attractive.

That restless thing kicked at her, swelling up like a high tide about to break and swallow the shoreline—

Michaela pulled out her cell phone with a hand that was *absolutely not* shaking, and, if it was, it was obviously because of the wind chill and nothing else, and called Terrence.

It went straight to his voicemail. Again.

"Hi sweetheart, it's me!" she all but sang into the phone, and she could hear her voice was much too high and certainly too loud as Jesse swung into the driver's seat next to her. It got worse when he slammed his door shut, because then they were trapped there. The two of them. In the muted quiet of the SUV's interior.

This time, Michaela knew exactly what it was that danced over her skin, making her stiffen. Pure, unadulterated panic.

"So the strangest thing happened," she continued, talking into the phone even as Jesse turned that scowl of his on her again, except this time he was much, much closer and she could *smell* him, soap and snow and man, while their eyes locked. "There's a gigantic snowstorm coming in and everything's shutting down, which means I could be stuck here for days if I don't drive out now. And luckily, there's this guy—"

"I'm sure that's a great comfort to your fiancé," Jesse muttered, still holding her gaze with his, even as he swiped that hat off of his head and let his dark-blonde hair do what it would. "As it would be to anyone. Some random guy."

"—this friend of the family—"

"I grew up in Billings. I'm not from Marietta. Your aunt knows my relatives but she doesn't know me, personally, from a can of paint."

"—this weird, socially awkward guy who might or might not be some kind of questionable painter," she said tartly, and had to remind herself she was leaving a message, especially when Jesse's hard mouth kicked up a little bit in one corner. Just the littlest bit, and yet her heart soared as if she'd won some kind of Olympic event. "He and I are going to drive home. That sounds insane but really, it's only about ten hours or so." Jesse's brows lifted as if that was funny. "I looked it up," she told Terrence. She was definitely talking to Terrence. "So I'll see you in ten hours! Yay!"

Michaela ended the call, and she should have turned away then, clearly. She had no idea why she just sat there, practically nose to nose with this man, as if neither one of them had anything better to do. As if this was at all safe, this *thing* she refused to acknowledge was swirling around in what little space was between them.

"You just said 'yay,'" he pointed out, maybe five or six thousand years later. "It was like a verbal emoticon, except scarier."

She lifted one shoulder and dropped it in a manner someone else might have called slightly belligerent, had they been nearby. But no one was. It was only the two of them, tucked away inside this SUV while the weather turned dangerous on the other side of the dashboard and the far savvier citizens of Marietta, Montana, stayed locked away inside their warm and cozy homes.

"I'm excited."

"You were leaving a voicemail message. At least, I hope that's what you were doing. Or that was a pretty spectacularly lame conversation you were having."

"Is the issue here that I said the word 'yay' or that you feel qualified to judge the level of my excitement, for some reason?" Michaela asked, and she could feel how edgy her smile had become. "Because guess what? You're a guy I bought in a bar. You don't have the slightest idea what excites me."

Jesse Grey stopped scowling then.

Right about the time her heart stopped beating, then kicked in again, like a gong.

A loud, low gong that made the whole world seem to dance and shimmer for a moment there, as if the threat of a Montana snowstorm was the least of its problems.

"I'll keep that in mind," he said, in that low, faintly rough voice of his, as if he knew. Every too hot, too liquid, too damning part of her that was still dancing, still lost in that shimmer. That low, insistent tug that was beginning to worry her just the littlest bit. That dark bloom of pure fire that was consuming her alive, right there where she sat. Every last dream she'd had about him over the course of her very long, very restless night in her aunt's spare bedroom with her mother in the twin bed across the pink carpet. As if he could see it all like stains, marking her up and making her that obvious, that ridiculous.

That doomed.

"You can do that while you drive," she threw back at him because if she didn't speak, she was afraid something much, much worse would happen than the breathlessness that stole through her and threatened... *everything*. She couldn't allow herself to think about it. Nothing inside of her made any sense. "I'm going to take a nap."

Chapter Three

"I KNOW YOU'RE not asleep," Jesse growled an hour or so later, when traffic ground to a halt yet again on the stretch of I-90 that skated along the thrust of the Rockies, rising up off in the west past Bozeman, and then sloping down on the other side of the Continental Divide. It was getting dark and icy—or more of each, really—and they still had a ways to go before making it to Missoula, the nearest city of any size. The driving snow and bitter wind that rocked the SUV made that goal seem more precarious by the minute, even to Jesse, who'd been raised in this kind of weather. "I hate to break this to you, but it's harder to fake it than you might think. Men can usually tell. Consider that a public service announcement from me to you."

That right there was the problem with all of this. With this stupid drive. With Michaela Townsend herself. He opened his mouth to be appropriately dour and matter-of-fact and what came out sounded more like flirting. If he was a fifteen-year-old boy with absolutely no skills or game of any kind, that was. And meanwhile, this SUV that belonged to his uncle was filled with the scent she carried in her dark brown hair, of grapefruit and soft spice, the suggestion of the vanilla-scented warmth of her skin, and entirely too much of her tempting body within easy reach.

She shifted then, sitting up straight and thrusting her legs out in front of her as she rubbed her hands over her face. Jesse felt more than saw her toss a look his way, but she didn't say anything. She pulled her jacket tighter around her and blinked out at the deteriorating weather conditions all around them.

"I knew you weren't asleep," he muttered, because he was obviously insane.

"That must be why you're so successful," she said, in the way someone who really didn't know what he did or how successful he really was might, and he liked that, too. That she lived in Seattle and didn't know who he was. That she wasn't one of those women who came after him like so many bloodhounds on the hunt. "Your discernment."

"What is it you do again?" he asked. "No one said. They just mentioned your man Terrence was unemployed. Has been for a while, I think your cousin told me, nine or ten times. What's her name? The loud one."

"Missy, who is not loud, she's emphatic. And it's none of her business, or yours, what Terrence does or doesn't do, thank you." He thought she looked at him, though when he glanced at her, she was gazing out the window, a distinct line between her brows. "Terrence calls me a glorified office manager, which is close enough to my job title, I suppose."

He opened his mouth to make some crack, but something in the way she'd said that pricked at him. Maybe it was his deep, abiding certainty that Terrence Polk was more likely to undermine than glorify anyone. "What's your actual job title?"

She sat up even straighter in her seat, and he knew she wasn't going to answer him. "I solve problems," she said.

"You can get a job doing that?"

"Apparently."

She didn't expand on that. And Jesse couldn't have said why that very nearly ached, down in his bones.

"This does not look good," she said instead, after a moment or two, still with her gaze trained on the treacherous road outside the SUV. Her voice was huskier than before, and Jesse would have had to have been a saint not to respond to that—to feel it scrape over him in a hundred inappropriate ways it was far healthier not to think of in any detail.

And Jesse was a lot of things, but a saint wasn't one of them.

"No," he agreed, keeping his attention on the road and the rapidly decreasing visibility. It was far safer than what was going on in this SUV. Or inside of him. "I think we're going to have to stop for the night."

He expected wailing, carrying on, or some passive-aggressive version of either. Hysterics, maybe. Some kind of attitude or fit, anyway, from a woman who had pretended to be asleep for hours rather than interact with him. But the SUV was quiet, except for the rhythmic *thwack* and *swish* of the windshield wipers and the crunch of the tires against the increasingly snowy road. And beside him, he heard her shift in her seat. That was the extent of her outward reaction.

"By the side of the road?" she asked. Calmly, he was surprised to note.

"I think we're close enough to Missoula to make it," he said gruffly. "It's not great out there, but I don't think it's bad enough that we need to pull over. Yet."

"We passed Butte already?"

He'd thought he should have stopped at the former mining town when they'd passed it. But she'd been "sleeping" and he'd been irritated beyond measure and had thought if he just kept going, he could outrun the storm and have them halfway across Washington State before midnight. At the moment, that entire previous thought process seemed like nothing but hubris.

"About two hours back. Under normal conditions we would have made through Missoula already and be on our way into Idaho."

"Then we must be close," she said, in that same calmly enthusiastic voice she'd used on him in Grey's the night before. Jesse didn't know why tonight, he found it something an awful lot like soothing.

She didn't say much more as Jesse navigated the rest of the way into the outskirts of Missoula, the roads getting more slippery and dangerous by the mile. They skidded into the first motel parking lot they found with a VA-CANCY sign, and Jesse figured he wasn't the only one fending off the rush of adrenaline that they'd made it. In one piece. He shifted the SUV into PARK and blew out a long breath.

They grinned at each other then, over the kick of relief and danger narrowly averted, and Jesse was sure that was the only reason his chest felt tight. He rubbed at it, annoyed.

"I'll go get us a couple of rooms," she told him after a moment, as he let out another breath. She set about zipping up and pulling on her scarf and her gloves, and he felt the loss of that expansive grin of hers like something physical.

What the hell was the matter with him? He needed a hot shower and a beer. And a good night's sleep now that he wasn't taking up residence on the couch in his uncle's office in the back of Grey's. That had been his best option as far as a peaceful sleep in Marietta went. It was that or deal with his Uncle Ryan and Aunt Gracie, who were certain to ask entirely too many questions about Jesse's relationship with his father. *No thank you.* Or his cousin Luce, their daughter, who was two years younger than him and possessed of three maniac kids and a deadbeat husband she'd just kicked to the curb, all of which made her way too maudlin when she'd had a few.

Or worst of all, subject himself to his grandmother's

sharp tongue, because Elly Grey had never met a member of her family who didn't disappoint her deeply and Jesse was certainly no exception. More Calamity Jane than Mrs. Butterworth, that one, the cousins always muttered amongst themselves. He hadn't wanted to give her the opportunity to expand on her reasons for thinking less of him by the day. His grandmother was a woman best loved from a minimum safe distance, but Jesse was getting too old and too soft to bunk down on couches while avoiding the fallout from her version of a loving chat.

That was what the matter was, he assured himself—not enough sleep and none of it at all comfortable. Because he refused to allow it be anything else.

Next to him, Michaela had to shove against the wind to get the SUV's door open, and then she was dashing out into the sullen fist of the winter storm, bent nearly in half as she made her way to the neon-lighted motel office where the VACANCY sign still glowed and briefly lit up the side of her face.

And she was just as pretty in that purple glow, damn her.

Jesse took the opportunity to get a hold of himself. He decided it was because it had been a long time since he'd been out in a serious Montana snowstorm and maybe the soft rain of a Seattle winter had softened him up too much. It took getting used to, the full-throated howl of a Montana winter. But a few minutes later Michaela appeared again, looking slight and easily swept away, as she charged out of the motel's office door and through the driving snow back to the SUV. And he thought it was a little bit more than *winter* when he had to order himself to stay still.

She laughed as she threw herself back into the passenger seat and then wrestled her door closed, and he wasn't prepared for that. Or for that flush on her cheeks. Or the wild, gleaming sparkle in her bright, hazel eyes when they met his.

He didn't know what expression he had on his face then. He didn't have the slightest idea how he was looking at her, but he suspected the spiral of sensation he could feel working its way through him was hunger, pure and sharp and deep. And that it was stamped there across his face like a mask.

Her smile toppled from that ruinous mouth of hers, and the sparkling thing in her gaze changed, but what replaced it wasn't any better. Awareness, feminine and hot. It made the snow and the wind fade. It made the scent of cold that came off of her jacket and the melting snow against her cheeks seem to echo in him, making him want things he refused to acknowledge, here in a motel parking lot somewhere on the wrong side of Missoula.

"I have good news and bad news." Her voice was husky again, and this time, Jesse knew it had nothing at all to do with any nap, pretend or otherwise. He only watched her, aware of the way that hunger in him sat there on his mouth, in his face, deep inside of him, like a great weight. "The good news is that they have a room. The bad news is that they only have the one."

The fifteen-year-old in him turned an exultant cartwheel. It was humiliating. The grown up version of Jesse, the one who could have any woman he liked and often did, gazed back at her. Calmly. Cartwheels be damned.

"Are you worried?" he asked her, and he couldn't seem to keep himself from leaning closer to her. Though he was wise enough to keep his damned traitorous hands to himself. "Think you might lose your mind and jump me in my sleep?"

She looked as if she almost smiled, but thought better of it. "Does that happen a lot?"

His mouth curved and he saw the way she swallowed. Hard. "You can't be that surprised. Can you?"

"You can rest easy, Jesse," Michaela told him, and he imagined she meant that to come out easy and light. Funny and maybe a bit charming. But it didn't, and something dark and distinctly aware moved through her hazel eyes, and then through him, too. "Your virtue is safe with me."

IT WAS ONE thing to *decide* to share a single motel room containing what had to be the smallest, most claustrophobic king-sized bed in the entire universe with a man who practically reeked of sex and dark, needy things, because it was utterly irrational to do anything else and they were adults who made choices, not animals.

It was something else, Michaela was finding out fast, to

actually *do* it.

"Are you saving yourself for your June wedding?" Jesse asked in that voice of his that sounded insulting even when the question itself was mostly innocuous. Or maybe that was the look in his sinful eyes. "All dressed in white and accompanied by an entire defensive line of bridesmaids and some Snow White–type doves cartwheeling around your head?"

This was all Michaela's fault, she was aware. She'd started the discussion of virtue, out there in the cold. She'd understood that was a mistake pretty much as she'd said it, which was why she'd also been the one who'd ended that odd, endlessly fraught moment that had swelled between them in the SUV by announcing they needed to hurry up and get inside before they froze to death where they'd sat.

"They're expecting another ten to fifteen inches overnight," she'd said, admiring how cool and unbothered she'd sounded, despite the heat she could feel stomping through her, all temper and fire. But then, she'd long ago learned how to appear calm and cool under pressure, no matter how she might have felt inside. It was one of the major benefits of her job. "The storm is only getting worse."

"No kidding," Jesse had muttered.

And Michaela had assured herself there was absolutely no underlying meaning to their exchange. No confusing, dangerous metaphors. None whatsoever.

Then they'd driven across the howling tundra of the

parking lot and around the back of the modest two-story building to park in front of their room. Jesse had curtly ordered her inside while he'd wrestled with the luggage—and 'wrestled' in the Jesse Grey sense meant he'd simply scooped it all up and brought it in with a minimum of fuss—and she'd obeyed him because she hadn't known what else to do and she hadn't much liked the hard, glittering look in his dark eyes anyway. And he'd kicked the door shut behind him when he'd come in with all the weather around him like a force field and then... there they'd been. Here they were. In a motel room in the middle of nowhere, in what appeared to Michaela to be a terrifying blizzard, but which the man behind the counter in the motel office had laconically called 'some winter weather.'

It was getting to her, she thought now, as Jesse waited for her answer with a darkly expectant look on his face, as if he could wait as long as it took if he had to. This single room thing was messing with her and she hated herself for it. It seemed so beneath her—so insulting, somehow, to Terrence and to herself and even to Jesse, even if she rather doubted he'd appreciate her concern—that she was treating this as if she really was some kind of latter-day Victorian miss. It all seemed so suburban minivan-ish, as Terrence would have said, that *proximity* to another man was making her hands shake and her knees feel weak, and worse, that her reaction to that was to clutch at her proverbial pearls and keep some distance between them rather than explore this strange reaction the way Terrence would have done.

Who makes all these silly rules? he would have asked in his languid way. *Who says we have to follow them? Sex is only love when we cage it and ration it. Sex is supposed to be fun. Why put all that baggage on it?*

Michaela had always agreed completely. In theory.

And she was letting Terrence down, Michaela knew she was, by allowing the fact she had to share a bed with this man—or maybe just the room itself, if he slept on the floor as she wouldn't *suggest* he do, though the tiny little part of her that was far more conservative than she liked to admit *hoped* he'd do anyway—affect her like this. Or at all.

The truth was, for all the thousands of conversations she and Terrence had had over the years about the elasticity of relationships and what love meant and how to stay committed and yet simultaneously free—Michaela had never put it to the test. She was always working too hard, or too tired, or she'd never met anyone worth bothering, or… something.

Jesse Grey she thought, should never be a girl's training wheels. He was more like a kamikaze ride on a stripped-down motorcycle, straight off the side of the nearest Rocky Mountain cliff.

Outside, the February storm howled and battered at the windows. The ancient radiator put up a valiant fight against all that commotion, but their little room was a collection of various drafts, questionable smells, and the supposedly king-sized bed that sat in the center, covered in a brown and orange bedspread that made Michaela think of fast food restaurants.

Or maybe she was just hungry. There was no food to be had, unless it came from the vending machine out in the frigid hallway, and she had already eaten three packets of faintly stale peanut butter sandwiched between bright orange cheese crackers. She thought she'd dream of real meals all night long.

Unless, of course, her subconscious preferred to explore the bounty that was Jesse Grey, stretched out across the bottom of the king-sized bed as if he lounged about eating Doritos while snowbound all the time. Hell, maybe he did. Maybe that absurd body of his was purely genetic.

It would have taken a far stronger woman than Michaela had ever pretended to be to overlook how this man looked in a tight-fitting, white Henley and those damned jeans. Even the fact he'd kicked his boots off by the door and was wearing nothing but a pair of socks on his long feet did her head in. She was losing it.

That was only one of the many reasons she was sitting in the uncomfortable pleather armchair near the window. And none of the other reasons made her feel anything but small and teenaged and embarrassing.

"Have you drifted off into a wedding coma?" Jesse asked, and she realized she hadn't answered him. Instead, she'd been staring at him for God knew how long, bright orange cracker dust all over her fingers and who only knew what expression on her face. "I hear that happens. Someone says the word *wedding* and you hear organ music in your head, think about a white dress that looks like a giant wedding cake, and lapse into a dissociative state. Right?"

"Don't be ridiculous." She'd morphed from pearl-clutching Victorian to starchy schoolmarm and that, too, was humiliating. She felt a heat like tears prick at the backs of her eyes, and thought she'd actually rather throw herself out into the grip of the storm than *weep* in front of this man. "Terrence and I are getting married at the courthouse, by ourselves. No white gowns or organs, no fleets of bridesmaids in tacky matching dresses, and certainly no dissociative states. We're not even having a party, because why have a *party* to celebrate a shift in tax status?"

"How romantic."

"The point is the marriage, not the wedding," she snapped. She couldn't count how many times she'd said that since she and Terrence had announced their plans to marry. At least nine million times this past weekend alone, while her cousins and her aunts and her mother all stared back at her in varying degrees of dismay. "It's a practical exercise that doesn't need to involve anyone else."

"A wedding doesn't have to be a spectacle," said this man who, she was quite sure, likely broke out in hives whenever the W word was mentioned by anyone he might be dating, or even in his general bachelor vicinity. "It's about demonstrating commitment in front of people who matter to you. Otherwise you might as well treat it like a visit to the DMV."

"In your vast experience with weddings."

He shrugged, and how he could look dangerous while he did that, still sprawled out on the bed, lazy and unselfconscious and with a packet of Doritos in his hands, Michaela would never know.

"So that's a no on the saving yourself, then?" he asked, sounding something a little bit edgier than *amused*. "Given that you're so practical and all."

No good could possibly come of answering a question like that. And yet her mouth opened and words came right on out, as if she couldn't control herself at all. "I thought it was your virtue we were concerned about tonight, not mine."

"I'm a vestal virgin, obviously," he rumbled at her in that low voice that was all sex and longing and bad decisions made real. "My purity is of paramount importance to me and I like to advertise it, too. Hence the white shirt."

He was kidding, of course. He was even smirking a little bit as he said it. And that restless thing inside of her shifted, then. Flipped over and lodged itself hard against her sternum.

"There's nothing wrong with that, you know," she said, frowning at the cracker dust she'd transferred from her fingers to her thighs. "Just because we live in an age where you *can* sleep with whoever you want, whenever you want, with no consequences, that doesn't mean that people who don't should be treated like weirdoes."

She felt his gaze move over her face and told herself the

radiator was finally doing its job and that was why her cheeks were hot.

"Did you just confess to something, Michaela?" he asked, lightly enough. But when she looked over at him, she could see that bright, gleaming thing in his dark gaze. It moved inside of her like need. "Is that the kind of night this is going to be? I thought that sort of thing usually took a few too many shots of tequila and ended up in the usual ill-advised round of strip poker, but I'm game if you are."

"Of course not," she said dismissively, and she refused to let herself think about strip poker with this man, ill-advised or otherwise. Even for a second. "But don't you think it's absurd how much weight and power people give to something that really isn't anything more than a simple bodily function?"

She was lecturing herself, of course. She was directly addressing all that strange tension that still had her belly in knots, the heat and the longing that pulsed in her far lower, the tiny bed he was already taking up too much of, and all the rest. And the way he looked at her, she suspected he knew it.

"Are you talking me into bed or out of it?" he asked mildly. "As seduction techniques go, this one is fairly robotic and depressing. Just FYI."

"It shouldn't matter," she said, and maybe it was that mild tone of his that got to her and made her voice sharper than it should have been. Which didn't help anything. "It's ridiculous how much we tell ourselves it *matters*."

"I'm not going to have sex with you tonight, Michaela," Jesse said quietly, deliberately, and she told herself there was no resonance to it. That it didn't ricochet inside of her, then seem to swell and take over everything. "But don't kid yourself. If I did, it would matter."

She felt the sizzle of that, the deliberate burn, but she only shook her head as she stared at him across the room. She pulled her legs up onto the chair beneath her and wrapped her arms around her knees.

"No one who looks like you has sex that matters. Not all the time, anyway. It's statistically impossible."

"How cynical." He tossed the empty snack pack of Doritos aside and sat up, in one of those rolling sorts of moves that looked like water and yet made her mouth go dry. "And insulting, I don't mind telling you."

"I'm not trying to insult you." She shrugged, and took a sip of her Coke, and it was silly how needling him made her feel less off-balance. *Telling him the truth isn't needling him,* she told herself sternly, and hugged her knees to her chest again. "But it's silly to think that two grown adults can't share a hotel bedroom without it turning into some sexual scenario straight out of a low-budget movie. We're not animals."

"If you say so."

She counted herself lucky once again that she and Terrence had a relationship that had evolved past this nonsense.

"I thought maybe we could clear the air, that's all," she

said loftily, and she shifted in her pleather armchair, even smiling at him. Not quite with pity. "I'm sorry if that offends you. Terrence and I have a fairly liberal view of these things."

"I bet you do." He stood then, and stretched, and that was a whole symphony of unfair. That long, lean body. The wedge of his lower abdomen that showed when he raised his arms, packed tight with muscle and dusted with dark hair on its way beneath the low waistband of his jeans. The amused expression on his face when he caught her looking. "Let me guess. You have an open relationship that you both agreed to because that's the kind of liberal people you are, but it turns out only he ever takes advantage of it."

"There's nothing stopping either one of us from 'taking advantage of it,' though that's an unnecessarily dim view of things. That's the point."

"So that's a yes?"

She shook her head, and she told herself she really did pity him, this beautiful man she hardly knew and didn't *want* to know. "Labels aren't helpful. We don't try to own each other, that's all."

And Jesse laughed. He threw his head back and let it pour out, and it was like he cast aside the entire winter that easily. Then he looked at her again, still laughing. "Then what's the point?"

Michaela blinked. "What do you mean?"

"Why bother?" He tugged his Henley up and over his head, sweeping it off and tossing it on the bed, and the world shimmered all around that remarkable chest of his, sculpted to hard male perfection. "The world is filled with casual people and casual relationships. Fair weather friends and easy betrayals. Why bother marrying the guy who's just another disposable piece of merchandise, indistinguishable from the rest?"

"Because we're adults who don't need to stamp brands on each other like we're cattle, for one thing."

"That's why you're not wearing an engagement ring?"

Michaela curled her bare left hand into a fist and hated that she did it, as if it told him too much about the darkest, most hidden things in her she refused to admit were there. She'd excised them, damn it. Or she'd tried.

"I don't need an archaic display of ownership to make other people feel comfortable about my private, personal commitments," she gritted out. "Also, I'm not a cow."

"That doesn't sound like adulthood," Jesse told her, though what she saw was that perfect abdomen of his, that magnificent chest, burned deep into her brain. Maybe forever more, like the kind of brand she'd always been so sure she didn't want. And he wasn't laughing anymore. "That sounds like bullshit. A whole lot of rationalization to explain away not wanting to actually settle down and make a real promise with real consequences if it's broken. Fuck that, Michaela. If you choose to spend the rest of your life with one person, that's the whole goddamned point. That person. Only them. Forever. Or you might as well not bother."

And it wasn't until he'd slammed the bathroom door behind him that she realized he'd stalked off at all. She heard the shower come on, and Michaela sat there in her pleather armchair for a very long time without moving. Without breathing.

Without admitting to herself she was more concerned about the fact Jesse was naked *right this minute* on the other side of the flimsy door than she was about the fact he'd just delivered what felt like a body blow. He'd echoed things she hadn't ever wanted to admit she'd felt, down deep in the darkest recesses of her soul, and she didn't know how to shove them back where they belonged.

It was the storm, she told herself then, still frozen in place.

It was only the storm and when it passed, the way all storms eventually did, she'd look back on this strange night with a strange man she'd probably never see again and find it *hilarious* that he'd managed to make her so emotional. She and Terrence would laugh and laugh, and then they'd go right ahead and have the exact life they'd decided they wanted, open and rational and free. Because *that* was the point. What the two of them wanted their life to look like, not what some too pretty and too rich bad boy with a chip on his shoulder thought about it when he didn't know a damned thing about either one of them.

Michaela told herself she'd never been more certain of anything in her life.

Chapter Four

GETTING NAKED WAS maybe not the best plan, Jesse conceded, leaning his head against the tiled wall of the motel bathroom and letting the hot water punish him. His body viewed that as a logical extension of the conversation he'd just *almost* been having about sex, and that was impossible. There would be no such *extensions*.

Jesse didn't poach. Ever. He was religious about it.

There were millions of women out there without men—no need to tangle himself up, even momentarily, with one who was taken. Even if the man in question was Terrence Polk, who was wholly unworthy of the term "man." And especially when the woman claimed her existing relationship was "open"—because if there was one thing Jesse knew about relationships, it was that they were always more complicated than they appeared, even to the people inside them.

He'd found that out the hard way, hadn't he?

Years had gone by, and he still didn't know who he was

more pissed at: his loser father for doing what he always did, or Angelique, his once-upon-a-time girlfriend, for letting Billy do it to her. He didn't care that they were married now, with little twin girls he'd never met. He didn't care how many of his relatives assured him Billy was a changed man, that Angelique and the girls had proved to be a good influence on him—the good influence his previous two wives, three grown children, and innumerable mistresses had failed to provide, apparently.

"Your father feels awful about the whole thing," his cousin Luce had told him as they conducted their Grey Family Pity Party in the corner of the saloon his first night in Marietta, before she'd succumbed to the urge to sing along, far too loudly and pointedly, to angsty Miranda Lambert break up songs on the jukebox. Which was when Jesse had decided to bunk down in his uncle's office, because he had no desire to live out any more country songs. "Or so I hear."

Jesse had shrugged. Barely. "Good."

"Popular family opinion is that you're turning into Uncle Jason," Luce had continued, smirking. "I hope that doesn't mean you end up slinging drinks to beat up cowboys, never to smile again, Jesse. That would be a waste. Besides, I think Reese Kendrick has the Being Jason's Sparkly Apprentice thing covered."

Jesse hadn't spared a glance for Reese there behind the bar, who nobody would dare call "sparkly" to his face. Not if they wanted to keep their own in one piece. The slightly older man was probably more of a favored child to Jason than any of his uncle's long absent and possibly estranged daughters were, at this point. And Jesse had been well aware Luce had been poking at him to avoid talking about her own bad romantic choices, in the time-honored fashion of every single member of his family since the dawn of time. Still.

"Here's the thing," he'd said, and he hadn't bothered to ratchet back the threat in his voice or the look he knew was probably all over his face. Luce was family. She could take it. "I brought my girlfriend home for Christmas three years ago and when I left on New Year's Day, she was hooking up with my father. I'm thrilled they've carved out some kind of happily ever after from such an auspicious beginning. I salute them, I do. But no amount of secondhand reporting about how sad they are is going to change the sordid little facts, is it?"

"Your heart is a stone, Jesse," Luce had said, grinning. "We'll be spinsters together forever. Doesn't that sound fantastic?"

Jesse had rolled his eyes. "I'd rather prop up the bar in this tiny little town. With my face."

But that was the thing, he thought now, using up all the hot water in the middle of a blizzard, somewhere in Montana. Being sorry about things was great, but it didn't change anything. It certainly didn't fix anything. And if people couldn't handle the consequences of their choices, well, maybe they should have made better ones.

"Not my problem," he muttered as he wrenched off the faucets and reached for one of the thin, scratchy towels over the toilet. He exfoliated himself with the damned thing for a while, then hooked it around his hips.

Michaela Townsend was another problem, also not his. Her ridiculous life with that liar Terrence Polk was none of Jesse's concern and that "open relationship" nonsense had nothing to do with him. *Nothing.* The myth of the truly open relationship was right up there with unicorns and happily ever after, as far as Jesse was concerned, but that didn't mean he had to dive into that mess. Or stray anywhere near it.

So he had no particular explanation for why he threw open the bathroom door and swaggered out into the room, like a cowboy in a treacherously small towel, like he was daring her to put her money where her mouth was. Jesse didn't know what that would look like, anyway.

Michaela had moved from her chair while he'd been banging his head against unpleasant old memories in the shower stall. She was perched on the edge of the bed now, wearing thick, wool socks, oversized pajama bottoms, and a tank top. She hadn't removed her bra, and he found himself smiling a little. Did she really think the mere knowledge her breasts were unrestrained yet still covered might send him over the edge?

Then again, thinking about her breasts at all dragged him a whole lot closer to the edge than he'd been before, and the fact he was standing there, naked but for his towel, suggested he'd been dancing around on that particular cliff already.

"Getting ready for bed?" he asked. He didn't mean that to come out the way it did. But he couldn't regret it much when the husky rasp of it made her sit up straighter, those hazel eyes of hers widening and the hair she'd let fall around her shoulders bouncing a little bit, which would have been mesmerizing if he was allowing himself to think about her like that.

"Yes," she said, and then she cleared her throat, but that only called more attention to how hoarse she'd sounded in the first place. "I mean, yes, I thought I'd turn in."

"It's all of seven p.m."

She yawned. A big, long, high-pitched, fake-ass yawn, complete with a bullshit stretch to go with it. It was the worst acting he'd ever seen in his life, and she met his gaze like she knew it and didn't particularly care if he did.

There was no reason on earth he should find that kind of delightful.

"I'm extraordinarily tired," she told him, a hint of piety in her voice.

Jesse eyed her. "After all that napping in the car? Are you sure you don't have a medical condition?"

She smiled. "I didn't ask for your input, Jesse. How or when or how much I sleep is a topic I can't imagine should concern you at all."

"Yet here I am. Concerned."

"No need," she shot back. "Watch TV or whatever you

want. It won't bother me." That smile of hers widened, though he thought it was significantly edgier than it seemed. "I'm going to pull the covers up over my head and what you do on your side of the bed won't affect me one way or the other. Unless you plan to treat it like a trampoline, I guess."

Until that moment, Jesse had planned to sleep on the floor. Because *she* might think she was in an open relationship, but *he* couldn't trust himself to act all blasé and unaffected when a pretty woman was tucked up next to him. Especially in the middle of the night when, if his past exploits and regrets were any guide, he'd wake up horny and lonely and more than happy to investigate any warm body cuddled there beside him before he woke up entirely. Why take the chance? He had no desire to accidentally find himself a part of the lies she was telling herself.

But the idea that she could tune him out and sleep right through a night in bed with him—when there were, literally, dozens of women clamoring for the chance and that wasn't arrogance talking, it was simple fact—burned through him like a long, ill-conceived pour of really good whiskey.

It lit him up.

It pissed him off so deeply it very nearly hurt, and he didn't stop to examine why.

"No trampoline," he assured her, moving toward the bed. He'd bet she didn't know that he could see the way she dug her toes into the carpet at her feet, as if she was ordering herself to stay still while he approached. He liked that a whole lot more than a good man should. He stopped when he was maybe a foot away from her, and kept his gaze trained on hers as he reached down, unwrapped the towel from his hips, and let it drop to floor beneath him. "But I sleep naked. That's cool, right?"

IT WAS SOMETIME after midnight when Michaela finally gave up the charade and shifted over onto her back to glare up at the ceiling from the depths of her now much too hot cocoon of blankets.

She hadn't slept at all. Not in the damned car and not in this torture device of a bed, and *certainly* not after Jesse had displayed his entire naked body like that, so close to where she'd been sitting that she could have easily simply tipped forward and—

Michaela cut off that train of thought. Harshly.

That was what she'd spent the past few hours doing. Playing whack-a-mole with the host of terrible ideas and beguiling fantasies that coursed through her in an endless stream, one picking up where the other had left off, all of them featuring Jesse Grey and that mouthwateringly perfect body of his, without flaw, she now knew, from the top of his eternally mussed-up head of hair to his big, bare feet.

And all the acres and acres of pure masculine perfection in between.

She had obviously turned into a pillar of salt as his towel hit the floor, and to her eternal shame, she was fairly certain her mouth had dropped open at the sight. So that she'd been gaping at Jesse—at *all* of Jesse—like a slack-jawed yokel who had never seen a man's penis before.

You never have, a smitten little voice inside of her had whispered, as if in a church. A terrible shrine to the beauty that was Jesse Grey's naked body, which was something she could never unsee. *You never really have, until now.*

She didn't know what she'd expected then. Jesse to stand there until she applauded or laughed or, far more likely, threw herself at all that male perfection? Or perhaps she'd thought he'd take his bachelor auction experience to the next level and put on a little show for her—a little bump and grind, maybe, until she found a few dollar bills to toss his way? Or make some kind of unambiguous move on her—not that *sudden and unnecessary nudity* was in any way subtle—so she could deal with that out in the open, once and for all?

'Deal with that' meaning decline, of course, she'd snapped at herself, more than once, and sharper each time. *You're not touching this man. No way in hell.*

Why not? She had thrown right back at herself. Also more than once, and gaining in internal volume with each rendition. *Are you in an open relationship or not? If you are, the whole* point *is that you can touch this man or any man as much as you want, whenever you want.*

She'd cut that nonsense off, too, because it didn't bear

thinking about.

And naturally, Jesse had done none of those things.

Michaela had sat there on the edge of the bed, frozen into place while her entire body burst into a tower of flame, which she'd been certain he could see right there on her burning cheeks. But even if he had, Jesse had ignored her.

Completely.

As if nudity was so normal—his nudity in front of other people, that was, and for all she knew that was his favorite party trick—that it hardly impressed itself on him at all. And certainly caused him no shame.

He'd gone over to his duffel bag and rummaged around in it, as if unaware he was giving her an eyeful as he leaned down and fished out what looked like a leather toiletry bag. He'd vanished back into the bathroom for a while and when he'd come back out, had slapped off the light and the fan, leaving only Michaela's heightened awareness of him humming there in the room between them. Then he'd sauntered—*sauntered*—back to the bed as if he didn't care if it took him all night to get there, and had sprawled out on the far side of the bed with the TV remote in one hand and the other behind his head like a makeshift pillow.

On top of the comforter, with the suggestion of steam rising from his naked skin, though Michaela couldn't be sure she hadn't added that detail in, retroactively, as a part of the hysteria in her own fevered brain.

"Sleep tight," he'd rumbled, in what had been the jauntiest, most cheerful tone she'd heard from him yet. He'd even smiled. "Let me know if the TV is too loud for you, once you're in that little cocoon you mentioned. I wouldn't want to bug you."

And he hadn't even glanced at her again after that.

Which meant Michaela had no choice but to do exactly what she'd told him she would. She'd crawled into the bed, despite the fact his big, long, *naked* body took up more than his share of the mattress's square footage and had been weighing down the sheets and covers beside. She hadn't wanted to address anything involving his body, not its placement and certainly not its current state of undress, so she'd simply made do. She'd burrowed down as far as she could on the very edge of the bed, wrapping herself in the part of the comforter she could reasonably claim as hers and burying herself there, like an incensed burrito.

While Jesse had proceeded to watch back to back episodes of deeply stupid sitcoms, as if he'd been placed on this earth purely to torture her with tinny laugh tracks and the inescapable fact of his perfect, goddamned body sprawled out so lazily only a few inches away from her tense, angry one.

Eventually, he'd turned off the TV and climbed under the covers, seemingly unaware that Michaela was still lying there beside him as stiff as a plank of hardwood. But he didn't do anything but switch off the light, and then there was nothing but the dark of the room and the slap and howl of the wind outside. The wheezing and periodic clanks of the ancient radiator and, slowly, the heat from

Jesse himself warming up the bed they shared until it become unbearable.

Soon, Michaela told herself, he would start snoring or drooling or something—*anything*—unattractive, so she could find him hideous at last. Then, and maybe only then, she was sure she'd fall asleep.

But the minutes dragged on by and that never happened. Jesse simply slept. He didn't encroach on her space, and he didn't make any kind of advances and he didn't even snore, for God's sake. He simply sprawled there beside her, as unreasonably perfect asleep as he was awake.

She thought she'd never hated anyone more in her entire life.

"Stress any louder and you'll wake the neighbors," he said, in that low voice of his, all rough and tumble and much too close for her peace of mind. "It's like a fire alarm."

They might as well have been sharing a pillow. His voice was all over her, and from close by. It was terrible. It made every part of her shiver into taut, pointed awareness and stay there.

"I'm not stressing," she told him, trying to sound anything but *taut* or *aware*. "I, uh, had a bad dream. I just woke up. I'm sorry if I disturbed you."

She heard him shift around in the bed and didn't want to think about how close he really was. How easily she could roll toward him, or even slide her foot across the space between them and touch him. All of him. She reminded herself this was a king-sized bed, no matter how tiny it had seemed the more she'd looked at it all night, and it had more than enough space for two people to sleep comfortably without bothering each other at all. But she still entertained a fantasy or two of making a bed on the floor instead.

Only the fact he'd know he got under her skin if she did that—and that it would amuse the hell out of him—kept her from it.

"I'm going to share a little secret with you." His voice was a rumble in the dark, and it wound inside of her like a hot rope of light and heat, making her shut her eyes as if she could block him out that way. "I'm what's commonly known as a self-made man. Mostly people say that as a code to let other people know that I don't fit the usual profile. Guys like me who work construction jobs to help put themselves through college don't usually end up running the construction sites afterward. If they do, that's where they stop, but I didn't stop. I turned my after school job into an empire."

"This is all fascinating, I'm sure," she said. She wanted him to think he was boring her. She didn't understand why he wasn't. Why she wasn't drifting off to sleep right that second. "You have my congratulations, I guess? Are you telling me this because you want me to call you Emperor?"

She felt the bed move beneath her with the suggestion of his laughter, though he didn't make a sound. The sheer, dizzying intimacy of that struck at her, so hard it left her ears ringing and that same bell tolling in her limbs, over her skin, knotted low in her belly.

"I'm telling you this because it was quite an experience to go from the pure, physical straightforwardness of a job site to an intellectual classroom on the U-Dub campus," he said quietly. "My father was a salesman, so I already knew how to pick out a liar at ten paces, but shifting back and forth between two such different worlds really made it into something of an art."

She understood the sudden autobiography now. "I'm not lying."

"Not in any real sense of the term, no, because you're so bad at it."

"I have no idea what you think I'm lying about or more to the point, why you think I'd bother to lie to you at all," Michaela said, still with her eyes shut tight because any minute, surely, that would make him disappear. "I'm glad you think highly of yourself. Confidence is great and probably really useful in your line of work. But I don't think about you at all."

She felt a shift in the bed and then a dip, and then he was right there beside her, that long body of his making hers slide toward him in a sudden, alarming way, and her eyes snapped open to find him propped up on one arm.

Right.

There.

That time, she heard as well as felt the little laugh he let out. "Liar."

He sounded very male and entirely too satisfied, and Michaela had to battle herself to keep from either venting her spleen all over him or worse, flinging herself backward to get out of his range. Either one would prove his point for him.

She held herself still. Very, very still, sort of on her side and sort of still on her back, and afraid to move at all lest she accidentally roll right into him. But not immediately springing into action to get away from him had its own issues. Like the fact her heart was beating too hard against the inside of her chest. Much too hard. She was terrified he could hear it.

"What would I have to stress out about, anyway?" she asked him, all of that tension in her voice. "It's the middle of the night and we could be waiting out the snowstorm in a whole lot less comfort than this. Like in a car by the side of the road, risking hypothermia. Since we're not, I couldn't possibly be more relaxed if I tried."

But he didn't answer. And tragically, Michaela's eyes adjusted to what little light there was and she could see him again. That gorgeous face of his and those decadent eyes, so intent on what he was doing. On her. So narrowly focused. He reached over with his free hand and he did it so slowly she could have moved out of the way at any point. She could have batted his finger away. She could have stopped him with a single word.

She didn't do anything. She only watched in a kind of awe as his hand moved closer to her.

Awe and something else that curled deep inside her like a thick, black smoke.

He didn't speak. He moved his hand to her shoulder where it poked out from beneath the comforter and she didn't understand what he was doing. What that faint touch was. Almost like a tickle, if smoother, and she shuddered. There was no chance to hide it or repress it, and only once she realized he could see her shudder did Michaela realize her tank top strap had migrated down her arm and he was smoothing it back into place.

He was concentrating on his task with a ferocity that made that first shudder kick over into another, and still he took his time. He moved the strap into position and then he ran his fingers down the front of it, just an unobjectionable inch or so then back again, to make it lie flat.

If it had been her mother, her cousin, someone she worked with, anyone else, she wouldn't have cared. If it had been anywhere else but in this bed, where she couldn't make herself forget he was completely naked, she doubted she'd even have noticed so innocuous a touch. If he was even slightly less beautiful, less... *Jesse,* maybe it really would have been innocuous. There were a thousand ways this could be a perfectly nonchalant, unmemorable moment between two people who felt nothing for each other, and Michaela was sure every last one of them shot through her in that instant.

But there was nothing the least bit nonchalant about that hard, hungry look on his face when he raised it, at last, to hers. Michaela forgot how to breathe. She forgot how to function. Her shoulder had taken on a bright red, burning pulse of its own and she was fairly sure she'd forgotten her own name.

Hers. His. Everything but the tension that crackled between them and seemed to set the dark on fire.

"Tell me, Michaela." And his voice. That *voice*. Like he was buried deep inside of her already, God help her. "Exactly how open is this liberal relationship of yours?"

Chapter Five

"No," she said abruptly. And then again, and far rougher, "*no*. I can't."

Michaela didn't know who was more surprised. Her or Jesse.

She moved, then. She pulled herself away from him, from the hunger she could see on his face as easily as she could taste it inside of her and from the echoing pull of it deep within. She hurled herself away until she was sitting up with her back to the headboard and a nice, healthy space between her and this man who tempted her more than she'd realized she could ever be tempted.

By anyone or anything.

Jesse didn't say a word. He didn't come after her. He simply stayed where he was, propped up on his side with the better part of his impossibly beautiful and, she was all too aware, completely naked body tucked away beneath the covers. The radiator cranked out heat in hisses and clanks from the corner, or maybe that was Michaela's own pulse, making that mighty racket.

It took her much, much longer than she thought it should to get her breathing under control. She gave up on regulating her body temperature. It was a lost cause, clearly, unless she wanted to strip off all her layers and… she didn't. She really didn't want to do that. She had no idea what would be left of her if she did.

"So maybe the relationship is not so open, then," Jesse murmured after what could easily have been hours. Days. The judgment she searched his face and couldn't find was there in his voice, and it made her tense. "Shocker."

"I get that you have a burning need to make me into a liar here," she threw at him, with maybe a little more aggression than necessary. Or maybe not. *She* wasn't the naked person in the room. *She* hadn't done the touching. "But that's your personal stuff coming out, I think. I'm not a liar and incidentally? Having someone call you one repeatedly isn't exactly the most charming thing in the world."

"I didn't realize I was trying to be charming."

"Probably because pigs would fly first."

"Michaela." He waited until her gaze inched to his. "I don't understand the problem."

And she felt as if there was something wrapped tight around her throat, cutting off her words. Her air.

"There's no problem." Because she was a grown woman or she was supposed to be one. An adult. Not an immature child, prostrate to the whim of any feeling that stamped through her. She'd always believed that. "Just because my relationship is open, that doesn't mean I'm required to mess around with every man I meet who isn't my fiancé."

"Of course not." But that didn't sound like a concession and sure enough, his hard gaze didn't shift from hers at all. "How many men have you messed around with, would you say? Just give me a ballpark estimate. Five? Ten? Fifteen or more?"

She felt her mouth fall open slightly, just slightly, and that told her any number of things she'd prefer not to know about herself. Things that until this very moment, she'd thought were outdated vestiges of the person she'd been told she ought to be as a child. Little ghosts of someone else, amusing in their way, but nothing at all to do with who she really was.

Here, now, she saw that she'd been kidding herself. They weren't ghosts at all. And they didn't belong to someone else, they were hers. And the very idea of *messing around* with five, ten, *any* men while she and Terrence were together made her feel faintly sick to her stomach.

And that meant she had no idea who the hell she was, after all.

"I don't think I'm going to answer that," she told Jesse with every inch of that calm she'd worked years to perfect. "It's absolutely none of your business."

Neither was the chaos inside of her.

"Maybe it was none of my business before," he agreed. "But now? It's critical."

"And why is that?" She heard the kick of temper in her voice and could have reined it in, but she didn't. "Because you have a hard-on and no place to put it?"

"I have hands, thank you," he said reprovingly, which was not a visual Michaela needed just then. "And, also, I'm not twelve."

"And it still has nothing to do with you."

"Let me tell you what I think."

"I'm going to let you in on a little secret, Jesse. I don't care what you think."

"Right. That's why you're staring at me like that, haunted and wide-eyed. That's why you shudder every time I touch you. That's why your voice keeps cracking every time you say something to me." He smiled, and it was the fact of that soft smile on such a hard mouth that did her head in. It made something seem to fall apart inside of her, like a building simply crumbling from the inside out, there one minute and the next, only dust. "What I don't understand is why a woman in a wide-open relationship would pretend she's not feeling an attraction like this, that's so fucking obvious it could light up the whole of Western Montana. Even in the middle of a blizzard."

Michaela pulled in a shaky breath, then let it out again. But the mess inside of her didn't go away. The clawing thing at her throat didn't ease. And she was either honest with herself or she wasn't.

"Fine," she said, because she wasn't a liar, damn it. No matter how much easier it would have been to lie just then—to both of them. "You're right."

He didn't smile. But the gleam in his eyes was so potent it almost hurt to look at him. "I'm right about a lot of things, generally. But you might want to narrow that down."

She lifted her hands up and then dropped them, letting her palms smack against the legs she'd drawn up against her—and she was perfectly well aware that she was basically barring herself off from him. That it was a defensive posture that told him more of the things he already seemed to know.

But there was no helping that, either.

"You said we weren't going to sleep together tonight," she reminded him. "Did you forget?"

"If I have to explain to you the long and varied and straight up fascinating stretch of road between not touching at all and actually having intercourse with someone," he practically drawled, and *potent* shifted into something so greedy and so hot it felt like a kick between her legs, "it's going to make me cast a lot of aspersions on the state of your sex life, Michaela. Is that what you're going for?"

Michaela decided, right then and there, to stop pretending she had any idea what she was doing here. Jesse was right. She'd never taken advantage of the loose boundaries in her relationship before. She'd never had the time and, honestly, she'd never been tempted. It had been awfully easy to sit around talking about how she'd act in the abstract, with no idea that it could *feel* like this, but there was no use beating herself up for that now. Just as there was no point succumbing to the heavy thing a whole lot like guilt or maybe shame that sloshed around inside of her. This was the first time she'd navigated this situation. Of course it was rocky.

"Terrence and I believe that no one is really monogamous, not naturally anyway, and that it's pointless to break up great relationships over things as silly as meaningless sex," she managed to say, feeling desperate and unhinged, ashamed and guilty, and she didn't even know *why*. But the fact they were sitting there in the soft, intimate dark didn't help. She reached over and switched on her bedside lamp, and if she were a better person, maybe she wouldn't have enjoyed the way he cursed at the sudden light. She certainly wouldn't have felt it leveled the playing ground, somehow. "What does one thing have to do with the other?"

He grunted. "That sounds convenient."

"It's practical," she insisted, though she'd never felt anything less like *practical* than she did at the moment. "Some people see betrayals wherever they look. How is that healthy?"

"Betrayal is betrayal." His voice was flat. Unequivocal.

"Betrayal is what happens when someone breaks a promise or the rules they previously agreed to follow," Michaela said. "But casual sex with other people isn't a broken promise or rule in my relationship. It's no different than going out for dinner or a drink, as far as we're concerned. What does it matter? It's not dramatic, it just happens sometimes."

"If it's like dinner or a drink for you, maybe it doesn't matter," Jesse said in that dark way of his. Judgy and snide, in her opinion.

"Right," she said, her voice arid. "Because you only make sweet, soulful, tender love. You connect on a higher emotional level, complete with poetry and promises, or not at all."

His dark gaze hit hers. Hard. "I'm not engaged."

There was no reason she should feel winded.

"Sometimes sex is just sex," she told him. "And Terrence and I have decided that our entire life together doesn't have to be predicated on making judgments about sex, that's all."

"But I'm getting the impression that sex isn't just sex to you. That it doesn't *just happen sometimes* when you're out and about."

"It hasn't as of yet," she agreed, because she was trying to be honest here, which was about *her*, she reminded herself sternly. Not him. Not what he thought of her. There was absolutely no reason she should feel as if she was losing ground—wholly surrendering, in fact. "But different people have different drives, different needs. That's perfectly healthy."

"Translation. Terrence Polk can't keep it in his pants but he's managed to convince you that he *needs* that."

She gritted her teeth. "It's possible, you know, that people who aren't you can think and feel things that make sense to them, without it ever having to make sense to you."

"I know Terrence," Jesse said, abruptly.

And there was even less reason her blood should seem to ice over, that it should thud through her as if one of the icicles on the back of her aunt's house had pierced her through the gut. She forced herself to look straight at him, calm and cool, and she didn't want to ask herself why that was one of the hardest things she'd ever done to date.

"Do you?" she asked. Mildly. "Then nothing I'm saying should come as a surprise to you."

"I was trying to figure out a way to tell you that your beloved fiancé is widely renowned as being completely incapable of keeping himself zipped," Jesse said, something flinty in his gaze and in the cast of his mouth. "You seem like a nice girl. But hey, no harm, no foul, if you already know. If you support it."

"I don't require that Terrence treat me like his confessional," she told him icily. "He doesn't need my permission to decide how and where he spends his time."

That was too much for Jesse, apparently. He muttered something and then he jackknifed up, tossing off the bedclothes and stalking over to his duffel. She had too few moments of staring at his astonishingly sculpted backside again, and then he hauled on a loose pair of grey athletic trousers.

He took his time turning back to face her, which gave Michaela a few moments to breathe again. When he finally wheeled around, he raked back his unruly hair with one hand as he settled that faintly grim gaze of his on her. He was beautiful and obviously pissed off, *at her,* and her body reacted to all of that as if he'd sung her a set of poignant love songs and topped it off with roses and a box of chocolates.

She'd never felt anything like this in her life.

It was terrifying and exhilarating, a physical longing that felt almost like some kind of quick onset virus, and it was one hundred percent *wrong.* She didn't care why. She didn't care what Terrence would do in her place.

Jesse Grey was not a trifle. He would leave marks.

"Go on," he growled at her. "I feel pretty sure you're meandering around to the real bullshit right about now."

"I have no idea what you mean. I'm sure I don't want to know."

"It means whatever convoluted reason you have in your head that it's great if your boy Terrence bones every last bimbo in the Pacific Northwest but absolutely unacceptable if you touch anyone. Especially me." He let that sink in, and then he crossed his arms. "I'm all ears."

Michaela realized she was breathing too heavily, as if she was flat-out running, when she still hadn't moved a single inch. Not one. As if she really was frozen into place where she sat.

"Sex that's just sex would be fine," she told him, and it was amazing how hard this was. But that was the point, wasn't it? If it was easy, she wouldn't have stopped things.

If it was easy, that voice inside of her whispered, *you would be a completely different person.* She didn't want to think about that. "This doesn't feel like that. You told me yourself it would mean something," she went on hurriedly when his eyes went unreadably dark. "That's too intense for me. Stress relief is one thing, but this feels a little more complicated than your average Swedish massage. Which would be great, I love massages, but complicated sex is something I can't do."

JESSE HAD NEVER been so furious and so turned on at the same time.

He didn't know what to do about it—aside from the obvious, of course, which it appeared was off the table tonight. And he knew, in some distant part of his brain where he was still a fully functioning person and not simply the caveman who would take her however he could get her, that this was a good thing.

Michaela Townsend was a complication he didn't need and shouldn't want, and so what if he didn't like the fact she'd been the one to say so? To call *him* complicated? That was pride, nothing more. Or it shouldn't have been anything more.

He told himself it wasn't.

"No, Michaela," he said then, holding himself by a thread and letting all of that hunger pound through him. Letting her see it. "It's not going to be like a goddamned

Swedish massage. It's going to be hard and dirty. It's going to make you scream. It's going to wreck your life and you're going to love every second of it. Believe me."

"That," she said, after another one of those taut moments where he thought the look in her hazel eyes, haunted and longing and cool at once, might kill him, "is exactly why it's not going to happen."

He made himself shrug as if he didn't care either way. "If you say so."

"I do say so." Her voice had gone sharp again.

Jesse shoved his other hand through his hair and then he blew out a breath, and then the sheer ridiculousness of this entire situation welled up in him and he laughed. And laughed a little bit harder when she looked startled.

"Did you expect me to burst into tears?" he asked, laughter still in his voice. "I think you're full of shit, let's be clear. I think your relationship is a disaster at best and a complete fraud either way."

Her chin rose. "Your opinion is completely irrelevant to me."

"Right. Noted. But we both know that you're lying to yourself, Michaela. And you're absolutely right, that's none of my business." He stalked back over to the bed and climbed in again, and then made a big show of pulling the covers up to his chin. "And the truth is, I don't care either way."

He heard her huff out a little breath, but he'd shut his eyes by then in a theatrical pretense of sleep, and he didn't open them again. He heard her shift, and felt the bed move a bit beneath her, and he thanked all the stars up above the blizzard somewhere that this was a king-sized mattress because he knew his ability to resist her—tenuous as it was—was entirely predicated on his not touching her. Not even by accident. Not even the slightest little bit.

Jesse would rather she not know that.

He heard the light switch off again, and then there was nothing but the intermittent enthusiasm of the radiator across the room. He might have imagined she'd drifted off to sleep, but he knew better. He could feel it.

As if they were connected in a thousand complicated ways that just pissed him off that much more to contemplate.

"Of course you don't care either way," Michaela said softly, into the strained, thick quiet. Straight into him, whether he liked it or not. "Now who's the liar?"

JESSE WOKE UP with an armful of warm, sweet woman and significantly less willpower than the night before. Neither of those things were good.

Or they're both really fucking good, the wild thing in him argued.

Michaela was sprawled over his chest, her face tucked against his shoulder, one knee bent high to hook her leg over his thigh. Jesse swallowed hard, ordered the most headstrong part of him to settle down, and took a moment to simply enjoy it.

To soak her in, like the freaking massage he was apparently not going to be enjoying on this accidental road trip.

She fit him easily and perfectly, like a key to a lock he hadn't known existed, and he'd have been a whole lot better off without knowing that.

Jesse knew he should shift her off of him. A nice man would do exactly that. He imagined she'd tell him she'd thought it was the loathsome Terrence, that she'd cuddled up to him out of habit, and Jesse would prefer to maintain the glorious fiction that this was all him. All them. Like they were magnets.

You're an idiot, he snarled at himself.

But then a phone started ringing, loud and obnoxious. Jesse had only just started scowling in the direction of the noise when Michaela's eyes snapped open. He watched her look at him—blank and sleepy—then had the distinct, if sharp, pleasure of watching her gaze fill with that awareness he thought might be the death of him.

She moved, then. She rolled over and slid off the bed, rushing to the phone that shrilled from a plug located in the center of the motel room's wall, convenient to absolutely nothing.

"I'm here, I'm here," she said, by way of greeting, when she got it to her ear. And then, "no, still in Montana. Good morning to you, too."

And Jesse indulged himself. He could have gotten up. He could have checked the weather situation outside, hit the bathroom. Given her the illusion of privacy in this tiny little room. Instead, he admired the way her pajama bottoms clung to her butt, and allowed his mind to drift into a fantasy of how the morning might have gone, waking up in that position with no clothes between them and certainly no phone call—

"You *insisted* that I take a few days off, and I listened to you," Michaela was saying calmly into the phone. Very, very calmly, which made him realize she'd used that same voice on him last night. *Interesting.* "Which is a good thing, because I got caught in a blizzard." She pulled the phone off its charger and turned, frowning at Jesse as if she could read his filthy mind. Although if she really could, he figured her face would have gotten a whole lot redder. "Yes. A blizzard. Though this is Montana, so they pretty much just call that snow."

She moved over to the big window that looked out over the motel's back parking lot and pulled back the curtains. There wasn't much to see. It wasn't snowing at the moment, but the morning sky was that same gunmetal color and the drifts were blowing enough fallen snow around that it would probably feel pretty much the same.

"It still looks terrible out there," Michaela said into her phone, "so I'd be very surprised if I'm going anywhere today." She looked over her shoulder at Jesse and raised her brows in silent question. He shook his head in equally silent agreement. They weren't going anywhere. "I have no idea, Amos. I can't control the weather." She laughed then, and it rolled through the room, through Jesse, a lot like touching her had done the night before. It felt like light. "I know. You might have to dock my pay for a failure of this magnitude."

She listened for another moment, then started listing off what appeared to be a set of appointments, from memory. She asked for another person to be patched in and then laid out what needed to happen over the next few days whether she was available or not, and by the time she'd finished her call Jesse understood that whatever job she had, it wasn't an office manager, and that she was obviously very, very good at it.

"You're not an office manager," he said when she faced him, crossing her arms beneath her breasts in a way he certainly wasn't going to point out only called attention to them.

"In a very real sense, that's exactly what I am." He waited, and she sighed slightly. "My last official title was Chief Administrative Officer. That means I tend to a lot of the nitty-gritty details of the organization, which isn't all that different from being an office manager."

"But you probably don't order office supplies and tend to the coffee."

"I have really, really strong feelings about coffee."

"You realize that the more cagey and evasive you are, the more I think you're hiding something, right?" Jesse asked. "Is that the goal?"

"Not at all." He couldn't read the look she gave him

then, but he could see the way she squared her shoulders. "It's called Burkeville. It's an organization that manages the fortune and interests of Amos Burke."

Jesse knew that name. Everybody knew that name. He blinked. "The computer guy?"

"His initial success was in apps, not precisely computers, but yes," she said, in the kind of even tone of voice that indicated she'd said this a thousand times before. "He left Silicon Valley five years ago because he hated what the Bay Area was becoming with too many guys too much like him, taking over San Francisco and treating it like it was part of their extended office. He prefers Seattle. People are used to random billionaires wandering around. They hardly pay him any mind. He has a few acres on Bainbridge Island where he lives and works, and it was a good move. He's much, much happier."

He considered that. "You were with him before he moved?"

"I've been with him since the beginning," she said, matter-of-factly, and her chin etched its way a little bit higher, which Jesse found fascinating. "I was his first intern while I was in my senior year of college. Then I was his personal assistant once I graduated, but really, that was because there were only two other employees and both of them were his roommates. They refused to get him coffee, on principle."

Jesse studied her for moment and then he laughed.

"Are you trying really hard to avoid telling me that you

got in on the ground floor with Amos Burke and you're rich?"

Her eyes glittered in the gloomy light. "I wouldn't use that word."

Her phone beeped and she uncrossed her arms to look down at it, before typing something out in a blur and hitting SEND. Then she looked at him again, and he could see she was bracing for something. Waiting for some or other shoe to drop.

"Sorry," she said. "It's Monday and I made them promise not to interrupt family time, so I'm sure they've been saving up."

Jesse took his time rolling out of the bed, and his stretch and yawn were real. When he dropped his arms back down, he saw heightened color high on her cheeks and a far more hectic sparkle in her gaze. It made him wish he hadn't pulled on his sweats last night, so he could have given her a real show.

"You look like you think you just confessed some deep, dark secret," he said. "I don't know what you're used to—" But he did, of course. He knew Terrence. He'd been a part of that hotel deal ten months ago that Terrence's bullshit had tanked. "—but I *like* rich women."

"I hear that's a thing."

"Michaela," he said patiently. "If you have your own money, you won't want me for mine."

That should have come out jokey and lighthearted, like everything else this morning, but it didn't. It seemed to sit there between them, rough and stark, like a declaration.

"Not that you want me, of course," he gritted out. "I'm not the massage parlor you're looking for."

She eyed him for a moment. "I would have thought that your whole growly, alpha male thing would rise up in protest at the idea that a woman didn't need you in all possible ways. Especially economic. I'd have thought that your whole purpose in life was to lord it over the little ladies and bend them to your will."

Jesse laughed again. "That sounds like a whole lot of obligation and pressure on my part. There are a lot of ways to need another person, Michaela. Not all of them come with the patriarchy and a power imbalance."

She didn't back down as he roamed toward her, and he liked that way too much, even though she was looking at him as if she thought he might try to take a bite out of her.

Well, she wasn't wrong. He just might.

"You were a lot less giggly last night," she said, as if she'd uncovered a deception. Her phone beeped again but this time, she didn't answer it. She didn't shift her gaze from his. He had no idea why that felt like a decisive victory.

"I have a constitutional aversion to bullshit," he told her. "I can't help it."

"I thought we agreed to stop lying," she said softly, but he didn't mistake the sharpness in it. "Or was it that you thought I should stop lying because I'd said something you didn't like, while you'd prefer to keep on merrily lying your head off? I can't keep track."

There was that wild thing in him that wanted out. It was part temper, part lust, and a whole lot of very dark and complicated things he had no desire to identify. Jesse stopped moving when he was a little too close to her for his peace of mind, but still far enough away that he thought he could keep himself from hauling her to him.

He'd managed to sleep with her last night without waking up deep inside of her, for which he deserved a freaking medal. He could stand in front of her and keep his hands to himself, too.

Or, at least, he thought he could.

"Hey, Michaela?" He didn't bother to hide the edge in his voice, because there was only so much he was capable of at one time. Her eyes widened, but she didn't shrink away from him, and he was going to have to take matters into his own hands—literally—if she didn't stop doing these things that made him so goddamned hard. His jaw tightened. "I'm not your fiancé or your boss. I'm the guy you actually said no to. I'm guessing that makes me the anomaly in your life. And guess what? I'm not the one you're mad at."

She jerked at that, and something indefinable sparked in her gaze before she blinked it away.

"I'm not mad at anyone."

"Sure you are." He wanted his hands on her more than he could remember wanting anything, ever, so he made himself step back. He made himself shrug, as if he felt nothing but lazy. The way he'd been about pretty much everything for the past three years. And definitely wasn't here in this motel room in the middle of nowhere. With her. "But I think we both know it's not me. It's you."

Michaela's lips pressed flat, and her phone beeped again. Then again. She glared down at it, then shifted that glare to Jesse.

"I'm going to take a shower," she said, very distinctly. Almost politely. "And incidentally, I'm running out of ways to tell you how wrong you are about absolutely everything without dying of boredom."

"You do that," Jesse drawled out. "But while you're in there adjusting your attitude, you should also probably try not to take too long. We should get out there and see if there's any food to be had around here before it starts snowing again." He nodded at her. "Unless, of course, you think you want another round or three at the vending machine."

She was standing much too straight, every inch of her brittle and crisp, and he was in all kinds of trouble, because he found that just as fascinating as the rest. He wanted to reach over and trace the pissy set to her jaw, that unsmiling press of her lips. He wanted to lick the *annoyed* straight from her skin.

"I do not," she said after a moment and another beep from her phone, "Want to eat another package of peanut butter crackers. Ever."

"Then you should probably get your ass in the shower."

Michaela looked as if she wanted to throw something at

him instead, maybe even the phone she held clutched in her hand. But she didn't. She tossed it on the bed, and then stalked over to her bag. Instead of pawing through it, she simply picked up the whole thing and carried it into the bathroom, shoving it down on the counter.

She didn't meet his eyes as she slammed the door, and there was no particular reason that should have made him grin. But it did.

"Oh, and you can buy me breakfast," he called through the door. "Since you're so filthy rich."

Chapter Six

WHAT SHOULD HAVE been no more than a two-minute walk in good weather stretched out into something more like fifteen. They'd stepped out into the sucker punch of the cold morning, both of them breathing hard and sharp as the reality of the chilly temperature made itself known. Like a full frontal assault. Michaela's eyes had watered instantly, the exposed skin on her cheeks ached in that cold, dry way, and she tugged her warm scarf tighter around her neck.

Jesse, by contrast, let out a sound that could only be construed as pure, male joy, and set off toward the motel office as if he found the weather exhilarating. He probably did, Michaela thought as she trudged after him, her boots—which were really more rain boots than snow boots, but were all she had with her—sinking through the icy crust of the snow and then down. And she tried not to think about how that sound he'd made was still reverberating inside of her, as if joy really was contagious.

"Walk where I walk," he called back over his shoulder, and she didn't want to think about the way his voice moved in her, or the warmth that seemed to spread out from deep inside her at that evidence that he was watching out for her—

Stop it, she hissed. Maybe even out loud, she realized when she saw the evidence like smoke in the air in front of her face. She concentrated instead on making his much-longer strides, and placing her feet in the holes he'd made in the snow that was packed several feet high in the motel parking lot.

It took some doing to climb over the massive snow-drifts and skid across the still expanse of the icy road to the only restaurant that was open for miles around, according to the same laconic gentleman in the motel office who'd been there the night before.

"Restaurant is a strong word," the man had said when they'd slammed their way inside, stamping off their boots and shaking off the snow and cold that clung to their faces. "They serve food, though."

"Do they serve food that can't be found in the vending machines?" Michaela had asked, and she'd felt more than seen the amused look Jesse had slanted toward her, as if he could see the orange cracker powder still stuck on her fingers. The man behind the counter had nodded, having apparently expended all his daily words already. "Then it's the right word."

The whole world seemed to be conspiring against her

when they'd gotten back outside, hushed and magnificently draped in white, making it impossible to think about anything but the surprisingly multi-layered man she was with. The way he'd touched her last night, so carefully—what was wrong with her that such an innocuous little thing should have taken over her head? She'd dreamed of heat and longing and woken up in a rush to find herself draped over his extraordinary chest. Thank God her phone had gone off, announcing the start to a new work week in its usual demanding way, and that she'd had an excuse to catapult herself away from Jesse Grey, his half-naked body, and *that look* in his decadent eyes. *Thank God.*

Because there had been a second—a split second between waking up and realizing she needed to answer that call—where there had been nothing between them but the flimsy layer of clothes they wore and the frank male appraisal in his eyes.

Oh, and need. Need like an imperative. Even more pointed and ravenous than the night before.

She could only imagine what he'd seen on her face.

The only sound as they walked now—and slid and jumped and climbed and sank—was their boots and their breathing against the endless carpet of white. There was the intermittent hint of the mountains all around them, tall and imposing, but mostly hidden by the weather.

And inside of Michaela, one avalanche after the next.

It had been a *relief* to talk about Amos and her work at Burkeville, and Michaela almost never talked about either of those things to strangers. She was fiercely protective of Amos and his privacy, on the one hand, but she'd also discovered through the years that it was better not to let people form their inevitably erroneous opinions about things they could know nothing about. Strangers thought whatever they wanted about her or about Amos and her relationship with him, and they posted about it all over the internet. Michaela certainly didn't have to give them any ammunition.

She lost her balance then, and had to throw her arms out to keep herself from toppling down—

And then Jesse was there in an instant, his strong hand at her elbow, holding her up.

It occurred to Michaela that she didn't think of this man as a stranger at all.

That revelation almost took her knees out from under her all over again.

She couldn't look at him, so instead she trained her attention behind him, realizing that what she'd thought was more of the oppressive cloud cover was in fact a sheer mountain slope coming down hard behind the small cluster of buildings on the far side of the road.

"You okay?" Jesse asked, that low rumble that sounded something like treacherous out here, in the shockingly intimate clutch of so much desolate white and cold.

"It's amazing that a mountain can hide so well," she said without thinking, staring up at the briefly revealed sweep of dark rock above the little roadhouse in front of them. "I had no idea there was anything there and then all of a sudden, there's a whole mountain where you least expect it."

She felt her cheeks heat up the moment she spoke. Terrence hated when she said things like that. He'd roll his eyes and mutter something in reply, usually about how her fanciful nature was one more indication that her brain was already mushy and silly—a consequence of both her steady diet of romance novels and her, in his view, mindless devotion to her job. She expected Jesse Grey—who was, by any objective standard, from his profession to his obvious comfort both driving and walking through a Montana winter storm to every inch of his hard-packed body, much more of a *man's man* than Terrence—to scoff outright and not try, as Terrence often did, to smooth it out later with claims that he was only looking out for her best interests.

She blinked at the stream of uncharitable thoughts. Where had that come from?

"Mountains are wily," was all Jesse said, tilting his head back to look where she did, and pausing while he did it. Not indulging her—listening to her, and something thudded into her at the distinction. He dropped his hand from her elbow and she missed it instantly, felt adrift without it, when she was perfectly steady on her feet. And couldn't possibly have felt his hand through all that winter wear and cold weather performance fabric anyway. "Always trickier than people give them credit for. You can see why some cultures assumed they must be slumbering giants.

Maybe they are."

Michaela didn't know how to respond.

Her throat felt tight and achy, and she was afraid the tears in her eyes that she'd been ascribing to the bitter slap of the wind had an entirely different source, suddenly. But Jesse started walking again, and she followed because it was that or something terrible—something huge, like an actual avalanche except all of it inside of her—right there in the snow-covered road.

And then she didn't have to worry about it, because they made it the last little way, and Jesse tossed open the door to the bright, cheerful heat within. A woman with a big smile, bigger hair, and an air of great frenzy called out a greeting as they walked inside.

"Anywhere you like!" she said. Michaela dutifully looked around.

There were coats and scarves thrown over almost every chair and hanging from hooks near the door, wood and mounted antlered creatures everywhere, big screen TVs, and a well-stocked bar. There were cozy tables near a roaring fire, big platters of food in front of the people sitting there with the smell of bacon thick in the air all around them, and the kind of buzz of accidental camaraderie that came along with finding oneself a pawn to the weather like this.

Michaela had never been happier in her life.

"This is perfect," she told Jesse, throwing back the hood of her parka and grinning up at him, heedlessly.

Recklessly.

He stared down at her, the suggestion of an answering grin on his hard mouth and something far too male and much too hungry in his dark eyes.

She flushed again, a sweep of crimson that rolled out from that gaze of his and flattened her, making every square inch of her skin prickle and come perilously close to itching. He made her want to tear everything off. And she didn't understand how he could *do* that. How he could stand there in about seventeen winter layers and *look* at her and make her feel naughty and dirty and naked and *needy* in a way she'd never imagined she could feel.

Michaela had never thought she was frigid or anything. But she read books that talked about *passion* and *desire* in terms she thought were fun, but excessive. Orgasms were nice, sometimes very nice, but not cataclysmic or life-altering. Everybody knew that.

But maybe not everybody was Jesse Grey, who could do more with a fully-clothed *glance* in a busy restaurant than some people could do with a wholly naked weekend retreat on a California king-sized bed.

She gulped. Audibly. And so obviously Jesse couldn't fail to notice it.

He did, of course. His gaze seemed to get both brighter and darker at once, or more sharply *male,* somehow, but he only inclined his head toward an empty table over near the big stone fireplace. And Michaela was racking up a long list of reasons to hate herself on this road trip, but the fact she all but *scurried* across the restaurant floor to take her seat—and to put a little distance between them before she burst into scalding flames where she stood—probably topped the list.

They unpeeled themselves from their heavy layers as they sat, and that didn't help anything. Jesse shrugged out of his coat and then pulled his fleece up over his head, exposing a strip of his ridiculously flat and muscled abdomen as he went. And then he was just a shockingly beautiful man with unruly hair he only raked a hand through, an unshaven jaw that should have made him look unkempt but really, really did not, lounging in front of the fire with his long legs out in front of him like an aspirational advertisement for outdoor living.

Outdoor adventures and then far sexier indoor ones, and Michaela had no idea what was happening to her. What was turning her into someone she hardly recognized, a stranger from the inside out.

You know exactly what's happening to you, that voice inside of her whispered. *Jesse Grey is happening to you.* But she didn't want to follow that line of thought. She was too afraid he could *see* it.

They ordered large mugs of strong coffee first and then, as the caffeine worked its magic, larger platters of home-style cooking. Flapjacks and bacon, farm-fresh eggs and sides of potatoes made three different ways. Then they settled in, both tending to their mobile phones and the Monday morning workday happening somewhere outside the veil of the harsh Montana winter. Jesse took a quick call that clearly related to his own business, and she liked the sound of his voice, quietly commanding and not the least bit blustery as he talked. There was the buzz of the other patrons all around them, the local news on the big screens, showing white-out conditions farther north, and beneath it all, the hum of something else. Something that vibrated like a tuning fork deep inside of Michaela.

Something she didn't want to identify.

But she knew what it was. *Contentment.*

It made her shudder, and she thought he knew it, too.

Their food arrived, heaping platters piled high, and they both dug in. For a while there was only the scrape of utensils against their plates, and Michaela thought she'd never tasted anything better.

Soon enough the first frenzy of eating passed, and Jesse sat back in his chair across from her, that gaze of his cool and assessing. Michaela wondered if this was the tycoon version of Jesse she'd glimpsed on the phone earlier. And if it was, which one was the real Jesse? The lazy, too sexy guy she'd woken up with? Or the one she'd heard order the person on the other end of his phone call to sort out a deal or prepare for the repercussions if he had to do it himself. Nicely, of course, but the steel had been there and very real. Or maybe he was both, she thought as she met that gaze of his, sipping at her coffee—lazy steel and commanding masculinity, all wrapped up in a sinfully wicked shell. That was Jesse Grey. Not a mystery. Just… too much.

"Why did your family think they had to buy me?" he asked.

Michaela allowed herself a smile that, if she was honest, was far closer to a smirk. "You were for sale, Jesse. Someone had to do it. It was us or that drunk woman who kept singing 'It's Raining Men.'"

His mouth curved. "You work for Amos Burke. Seems like he'd be a better, easier, and cheaper option than some random guy in a bachelor auction, if your family was that worried about Terrence and his prospects."

He said Terrence's name as if it was distinctly unpleasant on his tongue, and then took a swig of his coffee as if he had to wash it down. That shouldn't have been so… fascinating. Maybe because it was, Michaela spoke without thinking.

"Amos hates Terrence."

Jesse's gaze met hers. "Ah."

"What does 'ah' mean?"

"It means you can put your knife down, killer. That seems to be a popular take, that's all." He settled back in his chair, but the way he was looking at her across the table suggested he was anything but relaxed, even after she obeyed him and let go of her utensils. "Patterns are always interesting."

Michaela felt small and disloyal. If she were a good person, surely she would rush to Terrence's defense. That had always been what Terrence wanted her to do when it came to the tricky subject of Amos. He'd felt Michaela never chose him and that she didn't defend him very well, either. But the thing was, she saw Amos's position, too. *Because he pays you to see his position,* Terrence had accused her. *You put him first, but he doesn't do the same for you, does he? Or you wouldn't have to* ask *him to help you.*

And she'd never known how to point out to Terrence that it wasn't *Michaela* Amos flatly refused to help. That it was Terrence.

And there were so many complex layers to these issues back in Seattle. She had to defend Amos to Terrence and Terrence to Amos and she was tired of both, sometimes. She worked with a difficult man and she was engaged to a polarizing one, and she sometimes wished she could spend some time, somewhere, at work or at home, where the men in her life weren't the topic of conversation. Where she was who mattered, and not because she was expected to solve any kind of problem. Where people cared about *her,* not them.

But even here, in a roadhouse in a snowstorm in the middle of nowhere with a complete stranger, that wasn't in the cards.

"Amos hates everyone," she told Jesse briskly, when what she usually said to explain Amos was a good deal softer and more positive. More *eccentric genius* and less *misanthropic ass.* She didn't know why she couldn't seem to muster that up here. She shrugged. "That's what he does. His goal in life is to create ways people can communicate with each other fully without having to actually interact in the flesh. He's not a great judge of character."

"People with Amos Burke's level of success are always good judges of character," Jesse said quietly. "By definition. Or they couldn't possibly achieve what he has."

She assumed he was talking about himself, and couldn't have said why it made her feel so funny.

"That's what he hired me for." She shoved her hash browns around on her plate as if they'd suddenly gone uppity on her. "I deal with the people. Amos deals with the code. Everybody wins."

"You and he never...?"

"That's everybody's favorite question, of course." Was that bitterness in her voice? She'd never been *bitter* before, surely. She had no idea what was happening inside of her, and she thought that alone might drive her over the edge. Maybe she was simply too full, after a breakfast better suited to a team of lumberjacks. Or maybe the hash browns really were getting snippy. "No one can believe that a man and a woman could work together without years and years of sexual tension. People are more multi-dimensional than that, you know. They're not reduced to their sexual organs, careening around helplessly, humping each other's legs like untrained dogs."

Jesse blinked. Then grinned. "You obviously never spent any time trolling the local Seattle bar scene on a given Friday night."

"The answer is no," she said, resentfully. Why was she resentful? She put down her fork with a certain savagery.

"Amos and I have not only never hooked up, it's never been even the tiniest glimmer of a possibility between us."

"No worries if it was, though, right?" Jesse's low voice was too dark to qualify as *teasing* then. And that gaze of his had gone unreadable. Moody, but unreadable. "You have an open relationship. You could theoretically have Amos at work and Terrence at home seven days a week." His lips crooked. "But you don't do that."

That danced down the back of her neck like a touch, light and worrisome, then pooled at the base of her spine. It took her a moment to pull herself back to the table, back from that little trip to their bed last night and all the things she shouldn't have let herself say or do or feel.

"Sometimes," she said in a voice that sounded too obvious, too raw, "I have whole thoughts that aren't about any man at all. Much less any kind of sex with any of them. At home or at work."

That crook of his lips went lethal. "Like now?"

"Getting back to the point," she said crisply, ignoring her competing urges to throw something at him or maybe throw *herself* at him, "Amos is the stereotypical geek who never spoke to a girl in his life, until he made all this money and they fell all over *him*."

"So you seem like you'd be exactly his type. Female."

"Amos's tastes run to nine foot tall, one hundred pound gazelles who giggle at everything he says, do exactly what he tells them, and never, ever talk back. I'm like the annoying little sister who is and does absolutely none of those things." She smoothed a hand over her hair, feeling the static reaction that reminded her there was a whole winter outside, and beyond that, an entire world that had nothing to do with the things this man stirred up inside of her. "Plus, he likes it when I run his company and his life and that would be tough to do if there was romantic drama between us. We're purely platonic. We always have been."

Jesse eyed her. "But?"

"But what?"

"It sounded like there was a 'but' coming."

"Not from me," Michaela said and it was possible, she realized, that it all came out a little bit defensive.

Yet Jesse looked like he could listen to her forever, no matter how defensive she might or might not sound. "I'm guessing Terrence doesn't buy that?"

She knew she should shut this conversation down. It had never occurred to her before today how fluid and confusing betrayal was. She'd identified that having sex with Jesse Grey, while seemingly perfectly okay according to the promises Terrence and she had made each other, would actually involve a whole lot more than what she'd always imagined "casual sex" might entail. And there was no way that was good for her relationship. She might have talked around the subject last night, but that was the heart of it, wasn't it? Terrence and she had agreed on that a long time ago—nothing that threatened their bond was allowed, but everything else was fine.

Michaela had simply never considered how much

ground *everything else* covered. Or how slippery the slopes were, how uneven the ground, between what was fine and what was dangerous. She hadn't had sex with Jesse because she'd known in her heart that if she did, it would ruin her. It would ruin more than just her. It would be like a sledgehammer against all she'd held dear these last two years and the future she'd hoped to build.

But conversations like this were water damage, there was no pretending otherwise. Drip by drip, while Jesse watched her with those unfathomably beautiful eyes of his. While she said things about her life, about Terrence, knowing full well what his take was likely to be. This wasn't a safe space. Jesse wasn't a safe man. Not for her. Certainly not for her engagement.

She should stop this right now.

"Terrence doesn't like the demands on my time," she said instead. "I don't think he believes there's anything going on between me and Amos, really, but he certainly doesn't like how much of my life Amos takes up. Terrence thinks that if I'm merely an employee, I should have more time to myself."

Jesse shifted in his chair. "I want to take a moment to enjoy the irony here. The guy who doesn't believe in jealousy is jealous of how you spend your time?"

Michaela waved a hand in the air. What she did not do was mount a defense, which she normally would have. Which she should have. And she knew that later, when she was out of this confusing little space the blizzard had carved out of her life and away from this man, she would judge her failure. Harshly. She knew and she still didn't rein herself in.

"I think it's that he feels that I prioritize Amos over him," she said instead. She shrugged. "Which, of course, I do. Amos pays the bills."

"I would have thought the stock options you almost certainly have do that."

She didn't quite smile at him, but Michaela saw that bright thing in his gaze, mirroring back the look in her own eyes. She didn't want to think about what that look might tell him. What he might see.

"It's not as if I'm a wage slave," she conceded, after a moment. And then she continued, straying into territory she'd thought was locked up tight and hidden away forever. "Though it's possible that I might have given Terrence that impression."

"Did you, now."

"I didn't mean to lie to him," she hurried to tell him. "He made a few assumptions early on and I never corrected him. That's not lying. That's merely failing to clarify a few points."

"Or maybe," Jesse suggested, his voice as light as that look in his eyes was not, "there's a reason you don't trust him."

Michaela felt a kind of pressure in her head and a tightness in her throat, matching that constricted feeling banded around her chest, and still, she couldn't seem to stop herself. She couldn't seem to keep herself from talking. She couldn't even manage to break eye contact with Jesse, though he'd said something she knew she should disagree with. Forcefully.

Maybe, that same traitorous something murmured, *it's because you don't disagree with him at all.*

"The reality is that I love my job," she told him instead. "I don't want to argue about it, so I let Terrence think whatever he wants." That was the truth. It wasn't the whole of the truth, but it was still the truth. She pushed on past the tightness that was making her feel shaky. "Amos and I made it up as we went along. It's not as if I could slide over and do the same thing somewhere else. It's a position that was tailor made for me. By me."

"Is that what Terrence wants you to do?" Jesse asked mildly. Too mildly, maybe. "Go work somewhere else? Like, maybe for him in one of these unnamed ventures that you're sure will work out eventually?"

"Working together might be an eventual goal, sure," she replied, evasive even to her own ears.

"Has it occurred to you that Terrence knows exactly what you do for Amos Burke and exactly how much you're worth, Michaela?" His voice was still so light, so easy, but there was a ferocity in set of that jaw of his. In that look in his dark eyes. "I understand that to accept that, you might also have to consider the possibility that he's a little more of a con man than he is marriage material."

Michaela couldn't process any of that. She *refused* to

process any of that. She needed to stomp on the brakes before she toppled over a cliff here and couldn't climb back out. She knew it.

Jesse looked at her across the table that had seemed roomy when they'd sat down, but had shrunk since. And Michaela was so *aware* of him. She knew him, now. Not the person he was, maybe, after less than twenty-four hours in his company, but the shape of him. The physical reality of him, how he took up space. How the crook of his neck smelled after a night's sleep. The slide of his hard thigh against the tender skin of hers. The indulgence of his laughter, of his gruff scowl. There were so many different kinds of intimacies, she thought in something like a panic. So many competing complications.

"I don't think it's unreasonable for Terrence to want me to consider him the most important man in my life," she said carefully. So very carefully, as if everything hung in the balance. As if there wasn't a little prickle of awareness deep inside of her, telling her she'd gone too far and it was already much too late.

And Jesse didn't shift that gaze of his from hers for an instant, dark and hot and unflinching, as if he knew it, too. As if they'd been headed here all along.

"Is he?" he asked.

Chapter Seven

WHAT LITTLE DAYLIGHT there was disappeared entirely around midafternoon, and Jesse's cabin fever set in with a vengeance.

It had been a long, strange day. No surprise, after where they'd ended up in the conversation he should have known better than to have in the first place. Their breakfast had wrapped up in a significantly more subdued mood than it had begun. Michaela had tried to pay the check, Jesse had employed a little bit of sleight of hand to prevent it and pay it himself for reasons he didn't care to examine, and there had been far too much time over the last of their coffee to sit there and simmer in the mess he'd made with all those freaking questions to begin with.

And of course, Michaela hadn't answered the most important question. It hung between them, expanding and taking on weight and mass with every second she didn't address it.

Which was answer in itself. Jesse imagined they both

knew that.

Just as he knew he had no answer for why he'd put her on the spot. Or no answer he liked, anyway.

They'd made their way back across the snowy road not long after that, then settled into their snow day as new flakes began to swirl down outside. They'd each taken calls, pulled out their laptops, acted as if they happened to be sharing a work cubicle there in their little room. Michaela had made up the bed, as if that might divert attention away from the fact it was *a bed*. Jesse made surprisingly decent coffee in the doll-sized coffeemaker, which sat next to the TV. Sometimes, when they were both on the phone with their offices, one of them would step into the bathroom or out the front door for a little shred of privacy. They didn't talk to each other much.

You talked more than enough this morning, he'd reminded himself. *And since when do you want to* talk, *anyway?*

But that was another question he didn't have any intention of answering.

Jesse couldn't have said he got a lot done, especially when he'd expected he'd be back in Seattle and working on his problem job site today, but it was certainly a shift to spend some time with a woman who didn't give him shit for always being on his phone when he was away from the office.

You are messed up, he told himself then, glaring out at the cold, snowy parking lot as he ended another call to one of his project managers. Because the thought was insane and he knew it. He wasn't in any kind of relationship with Michaela. They were snowbound together, nothing more, and he thought maybe he should hold off on going back inside the motel room until he got that a little straighter in his head.

The last woman he'd spent any time with outside of a bed and therefore gotten to know at all was Angelique. Treacherous, two-faced, purposefully useless Angelique, who would have gone out of her mind in a situation like this. No spa, no magazines, no shopping. She'd have hated Jesse spending time on the phone when he could have been entertaining her instead. She would have complained the entire way to and from the restaurant, until Jesse had done something like pick her up and carry her, which would have been her goal from the start.

Angelique would have pretended to be mad at him for causing this delay, this incredible inconvenience to a woman who barely worked and thus had very little to do with herself whether snowbound or not, and he'd have had to cajole her into a better mood. Usually in a way that had involved sex. Eventually. If she'd felt he'd earned it. And of course, he would have thought all of that was fun, because it had been. *She* had been. Angelique had been crazy in the way some women were, when they thought beauty and sex were their only currency, and they wanted to make sure a man was invested. Hell, Jesse had been invested. He'd thought he was in love with her.

But handling Angelique would have been what he'd

spent the day doing. He wouldn't have taken all of these calls, or if he'd absolutely had to take them, he'd have been stressed out the whole time and then she'd have made him pay. He let out a long breath now, watching the cloud of it hang before him in the air, and tucked his hands beneath his armpits so he could take a few more minutes out here in the cold. A few more minutes without Michaela's efficient, professional voice in his ears, or the sight of her sitting in the armchair, typing furiously on her laptop while wrapped in a scarf and a bulky sweatshirt—about as far away from Angelique's seductive, throaty whisper and deliberately provocative presentation as it was possible to get.

Jesse was in so much trouble.

Would he have stopped himself last night? Had he been making a move or merely making a point? How could he not know?

Michaela wasn't free. Not even close. She was in an "open" relationship with a con man that even she didn't think was all that open—or not open to Jesse, anyway, which he supposed was some kind of backhanded compliment. Lucky him. And that was when she wasn't preoccupied with her own very high-octane and demanding job, something he, as someone who was equally focused on his own work, found as hot as he did impressive. And God help him, he wanted a taste of her.

He wanted more than a taste.

Jesse turned and eyed the door to their room, knowing the worst thing he could do was walk back in there, feeling the way he did then. She was warm and soft. The moisturizer she used was gently scented with vanilla and something else that drove him crazy. He'd left her sloped over the arm of the chair, her feet dangling and one arm thrown over her head as she talked through a set of bullet points with someone she obviously found challenging, something he could tell from her posture but not the cool, professional voice she used.

Which made him feel edgy. Needy. Very, very hungry.

He found everything about her way too hot, if he was honest. The dark hair she'd piled on the top of her head as if she hadn't given a single thought to it since she'd shot out of bed this morning. The jeans that clung to her hips with the temptingly low waistline he wanted to explore with his mouth. The same magenta shirt she'd been wearing at Grey's, layered over a t-shirt and why the hell was he risking frostbite out here, thinking about unwrapping her like his very own Valentine's Day gift? What the hell was happening to him?

When his phone buzzed again he decided it was divine intervention, giving him one last shot at not being such an asshole.

"Hey, Uncle Jason," he said, calmly enough, once he glanced at the screen and swiped to take the call.

But Jason Grey never said unnecessary things. Or anything at all, if that was possible. Not even a *hello*.

"Did you beat that storm?" he asked instead. "Heard it dumped on Missoula."

"It's still dumping on Missoula," Jesse said, scowling at the swirl of snow coming down from above, as if it planned to keep snowing forever. And what would be left of him if it did? He didn't want to think about it. "We had to stop last night when we lost all visibility on I-90. We're holed up somewhere east of Mount Jumbo."

Jason made one of those noises of his. It could have been commiseration. It could have been something else entirely, like incisive commentary on the harsh realities of Montana winters. The again, he could have been clearing his throat because he had a completely unrelated cold.

"What's the timeframe on getting back here?" he asked, the noise a mystery. "Still going to go all the way to Seattle when the roads clear?"

Jesse had initially figured he'd fly back to Seattle to deal with the little speed bump in one of his projects this morning, then turn around on Tuesday or Wednesday and subject himself to the big family dinner his grandmother was planning out at Big Sky the following weekend. It took a chunk out of his planned family time, but it couldn't be helped. Then the weather report had made driving seem like the better option, Jason had thrown him the keys to the SUV, and here he was.

Losing his mind in a dingy little motel room with a woman he didn't know well, but knew better than to want.

"Maybe another day in Seattle on the back side," he said now, like none of that was affecting him. "I should be back in Marietta before the weekend."

Jason grunted. Jesse interpreted that as warm wishes on his safe travels, there and back.

"Did you plan this?" he asked, before he could think better of it and stop himself. It was the cabin fever getting to him, he figured when there was no pretending he hadn't said it. Or the cold making his hands—and all the rest of him, for that matter—feel raw.

"I don't plan snowstorms," Jason said in his gruff way. "But they happen all the same. With alarming regularity in these parts, in case you forgot out there in the big city."

"I meant Michaela," Jesse said, already deeply regretting whatever urge he'd had to bring this up. He ran a hand over his face and tried not to imagine the expression his uncle would be wearing right now, all that incredulous scorn mixed with bone-deep grumpiness. "You're the one who entered me in that damned auction with all that crap about checks I couldn't cash."

"Oh, son." And Jason let out that laugh of his that sounded a whole lot like another man's shout, and promised all kinds of retribution Jesse didn't really care to consider just then. "I don't do Disney. If I'm the one playing fairy godmother in your little stuck-in-the-snow scenario here, you're in a world of hurt."

But of course, Jesse already knew that.

Now his uncle knew it, too. *Awesome.*

He didn't understand how any of this was happening to him.

Jason hung up on him, still laughing Jesse shouldered

his way inside the room, cursing himself for being such an idiot, and nearly ran straight into Michaela as she came bursting out of the bathroom at the same time.

He should have jumped out of the way. He should have done anything but what he did, given where his head had been all day—but Jesse couldn't seem to stop himself from grabbing her and holding her there, in front of him and too close to him, his hands wrapped around her upper arms and her pretty face upturned and *right there*—

"Your hands," she said, though there was a storm in her bright hazel eyes, hectic and wild. "Your hands are *so cold*."

"It's cold out there."

She laughed, as if there wasn't this tension winding between them. As if they weren't stuck here, pretending to ignore the raging chemistry between them. He didn't understand how he wasn't already inside her, and who cared how complicated it was—

But he did, he reminded himself. He cared. Didn't he?

"Really?" she teased him, and it took him a second to work out that she was still talking about the cold outside, and coming off of him like a scent. "I didn't notice, with all the snow banks and the slippery ice and the treacherous mountain passes."

"Let me remind you," Jesse suggested, because he obviously had some kind of death wish, or maybe he just wanted to torture himself.

He took his hand off of her arm and he didn't even question what he was doing as he reached down, then slid it up under her shirt and that bulky sweatshirt she wore, sliding his big, ice-cold palm directly against the soft skin of her belly.

Michaela yelped and jumped, then clapped her hands to his as if she wanted to pry it from her body, but he kept it there anyway. Easily. And then the next thing was they'd moved, or he'd backed her into the wall, and she wasn't making that high pitched noise any longer. And her hands were still on his, but she wasn't struggling against him, she was holding his hand right there where it rested against her skin.

And he could feel her tremble underneath his palm, as if it was rolling out of her from deep within.

She was soft. So deliciously, dangerously warm, and the heat of her poured into him, the contrast to his near-frozen hand electric. Almost painful. He let go of her other arm and put his free hand on the wall, right there near her head. He didn't step back. If anything, he angled himself closer.

Much too close to her mouth.

He swallowed hard, kept his gaze on hers, and moved the hand against her belly.

Incrementally. Experimentally.

Michaela shuddered. Her face flushed hot and red, her eyes went dark, her lips parted, and he was a goner. He was lost.

He was ravenous.

Her eyes were huge and the glossy, glassy dark made him ache, and he could see her pulse in her neck. Wild.

Fast. Exposing her and calling to him at the same time. He leaned closer, as if he might put his mouth on her neck, just to taste her excitement. Michaela tipped her head back, tilting that mouth of hers closer to his.

This was more than thin ice. This was insanity.

The images in his head were erotic. Pure madness. They wouldn't have to make it to the bed. He could have her right here. He could pull her leg over his hip and lift her up the smallest bit, lean back and drive home, and take the edge off, fast and furious. Then take her to bed when they caught their breath and indulge himself more thoroughly.

But first, he had to taste her. He had to taste her or go mad, though he knew, somehow, it wasn't a madness he could escape. There was no working it out of his system the old fashioned way, not with this woman. Not with Michaela. That one taste would never be enough, it might even make all of this worse.

Jesse didn't have it in him to care.

He moved his hand again, taking it slowly, deliberately, from that faintly rounded belly of hers and smoothing his way higher until his fingers brushed the scalloped edge of the bra she'd worn to ward him off last night. He'd never wanted anything more, just then, than he wanted to free her breasts and worship them with his own two hands.

And his mouth. And his teeth. And his tongue.

And she shuddered again, hard and deep, and he thought he might die if he didn't—

Michaela moved, then. Fast.

She ducked under his arm and she staggered as she moved back toward the bathroom door. Her phone rang, but she didn't react. She didn't even look in its direction. She stared at Jesse, and he thought he probably had the same look on his face, shell-shocked and sensual, as if he was completely destroyed and yet still strung out on that edge.

"There are only so many lines I can cross until I'm not me anymore," she said, and her voice was harsh and hoarse and there was a sob in it, too, waiting to crack wide open.

Jesse felt like a wild thing as he stood there, still so hungry for her it bordered on desperation, and he thought for a moment it might actually kill him. He was still keyed-in to her delicate scent, to the heat of her body, to the arousal he could see as plainly as if she'd written it in marker on her forehead—her flushed cheeks, her too-bright eyes, her shallow breaths.

"Michaela." Her name was like a song in his mouth, and he still didn't know what to say. Much less how to say it. None of this was okay with him. None of it was what he wanted.

But he wanted her all the same.

"This isn't *me*," she hissed at him, and then she went back inside the bathroom and closed the door. A quiet click, not a slam, and then the lock turned and he didn't know if it was to keep him out or her in.

And Jesse stood there in that dim little room with both

of their phones ringing too loud and too insistent from their far-off real lives where this never would have happened, need like a fist around him, clenching him too damned tight to breathe.

MICHAELA HAD NO idea what woke her that night.

She jolted awake, then gasped for breath while her heart did its level best to climb straight out through her ribs. She sat up in a rush, feeling wild and under attack, and clapped both of her hands to her chest as if she could make her heart behave with her own two palms.

It took one hard kick against her chest to remember where she was. Another to figure out *why*. That she was still in the same dinky little motel room, on this snowy side-of-the-road, somewhere in Montana, still nowhere close to home. The room was dark. There was only a fitful sometime-light poking through the curtains they hadn't quite drawn shut over the windows, and it took her much longer than that to realize it was the moon out there, high and bright.

She pulled in a breath and looked around, sleep still clinging to her.

Jesse.

His name was like a burst of sensation inside of her and she shifted against it, as if that might ward him off, and it took another long moment to realize she couldn't hear him anywhere in the room. She already knew he wasn't beside her. He hadn't taken the bed again with her when she'd finally decided it was time to crawl under the covers and put this day behind her as best she could.

"It's a huge bed, Jesse," she'd snapped at him, pretending she couldn't feel his palm against her belly all those hours later like one of those cattle brands she'd been so certain she wanted nowhere near her. But she could. She still could. "There's no reason we can't share it. We're not mindless animals."

He hadn't said much to her after she'd come out of the bathroom and managed to face him in the wake of their near-kiss. It had gotten almost as cold inside their room with the heat on as it had been outside, she'd thought, or maybe that had only been the air between them. They'd taken a grim march over the even more treacherous road in the bitter dark to grab something for dinner, had eaten in the same brooding silence once they'd hauled it back to their room, and it had been Michaela who had turned on the TV to find refuge in as many silly sitcoms as possible, and no matter if she normally hated that kind of thing. It was a laugh track or a lost mind. She'd chosen the former.

But it only meant when he'd turned the full force of his dark, brooding attention on her, she'd felt it. Oh lord, had she felt it.

"Speak for yourself," Jesse had growled.

It had taken her a long time to fall asleep, liked a martyred burrito wrapped up way too tight against the night—and against her own urges.

She moved to the edge of the bed now, scanning the room as she went, but there was no sign of him in the shadows on the floor. There was a leftover tangle of blankets near the radiator where he'd flopped down hours earlier and the bathroom door hung open, showing the dark and empty tiled room beyond. The clock on the side table declared it was three seventeen a.m. in neon green and Jesse was gone.

Michaela swung her legs over the side of the bed and got up, moving to the window without really questioning what she was doing. She didn't think he'd simply leave her here or, she was quite certain, he would have done so earlier today. She glanced over to assure herself his duffel was still on the floor. It was. But what could he possibly be doing at this hour?

She pushed the curtain back and saw a figure out by the SUV they'd parked in the lot out front what seemed like a lifetime ago. It was Jesse, of course, scraping the ice and snow from the SUV's windows, the moon dancing over him as he leaned over the windshield with that restrained male grace that made her feel… cottony, all the way through.

A wise woman might have gone back to bed and left a man who wanted to scrape snow from a car in the dead of the night to his own devices. She recognized that. But Michaela moved over to the door and swung it open anyway.

It was cold. *So unbelievably cold.* It didn't rush in so

much as seep against the frail protection of her thick socks, her pajama bottoms, and the long-sleeved shirt she'd worn to bed tonight as if it had been last night's tank top that had caused all the trouble between them. The sky was impossibly dark outside the moonlight and achingly, endlessly quiet in a way it never was in Seattle. As if there was no separation between them and the sky and the great universe hovering on the other side of the moon, all one tremendous stillness.

"Go back inside." Jesse's voice was low and yet held that same steel-laced command she'd heard him use on the phone earlier. "It's too cold out here."

She ignored him, but her body certainly didn't. It shivered awake in a hurry, her nipples pebbling and a rush of heat like a deep ache low in her belly. Michaela told herself it was the cold. Not his husky, deliciously male voice.

Not him. Definitely not him. It was the temperature.

"What are you doing?" she asked, rather than continuing to lie to herself.

He finished the side of the windshield he was working on and then pulled back, shaking off the scraper at his side. He took his time looking at her in that bland way, as if what he was doing ought to be so obvious it didn't require comment. It set her teeth on edge.

"I can see you're scraping the windshield, Jesse, thank you," she managed to say without letting *too* much of her temper bleed into her voice. "Why are you doing it at three-fifteen in the morning?"

He opened the nearest car door and tossed the scraper inside. Then he slammed it shut and started toward her, and she didn't know what gripped her then, as he moved. A sense of thick, pulsing foreboding. It was that unreadable expression on his face, that dangerous gleam in his eyes. The way he never shifted his hard, tight focus from her.

It was the way she felt inside, thrilled and altered. *Alive.*

Her toes curled into the carpet below her feet, hard. And she understood something then she should have recognized the moment she'd set eyes on Jesse in the bar back in Marietta, when she'd been struck silly at the sight of him—something that had never, ever happened to her.

Maybe it was the moonlight, reflecting off the snow and making the world seem ghost-lit and mysterious, but she didn't think so. It was him. Jesse. It was this insanity between them that had only gotten worse the more time they'd spent in each other's company, no matter how many increasingly desperate voicemail messages she'd left for Terrence. It was the fact she'd never felt anything like this before. It was the simple truth that she felt more for this man she hardly knew and had barely touched than she did for the man she was supposed to marry. And once she admitted that, once she accepted it, once she let it creep inside of her and take root, there was no pretending otherwise.

It had taken this odd, accidental vacation from her life with a man who knew nothing about her to understand how many things were wrong. With her. With the life she'd been living on autopilot for the past few years. With the decisions she'd made and the reasons she'd made them.

Michaela wasn't about to make any declarations on no sleep and too much forced proximity, to a relative stranger, no less. She wasn't sure she'd ever see Jesse Grey again, if they ever made it through this storm and back to Seattle, and she wasn't sure it mattered. But there was no way she could marry Terrence if she could feel like this about someone else. There was no possible way.

It didn't matter what they'd agreed. She didn't want to "scratch an itch" with Jesse the way she knew Terrence had with any number of other women over the past two years. This wasn't an itch. There was absolutely nothing casual about the set to Jesse's beautiful mouth or the rush of molten heat inside of her that made her stomach clench tight, and it didn't matter if it was only sex. If it was only physical.

Michaela hadn't believed she could feel this way. That anyone could outside the pages of her books.

And now that she knew better, she wasn't going to settle.

She refused to settle. Amos might not put her first. Terrence certainly didn't. But Michaela could. And from now on, she would. She promised herself she would, in a thick, hot rush of a vow she could feel all the way down to her toes.

But all of that was a problem for a later time. Conversations to have, a wedding to cancel, a whole life to change.

Right now she was standing on the doorstep of a motel room in the middle of Montana with the most beautiful man she'd ever seen in real life, who was looking at her as if *she* was the edible one. As if he'd like to put his hands on her again, and not stop until he'd slaked his hunger, like some kind of animal.

And she was supposed to be this rational, reasonable *human*—she'd prided herself on that and built a life around not feeling things so *deeply* or *dramatically*—but all she wanted was to jump on him and figure out what that wildness felt like, no matter what it cost her. No matter what it took.

No matter if it meant that she was an animal, too.

"Go inside," Jesse said again, even rougher, coming to a humming, electrically charged stop in front of her. "Pack up your stuff. The moon is up and the roads are clear. We should be in Seattle by noon at the latest if we get moving now."

"Okay," she said, but she didn't move.

He searched her face and he saw. He knew. She could see that he did.

"Goddamn it, Michaela."

But she wasn't listening to him anymore. She was listening to the exultant kick of her heart. To the soaring fear that had kicked her out of a dead sleep when she hadn't known where he was. To the part of her that only he'd ever woken up.

And she was wide awake now. More awake than she'd

ever been.

Michaela reached up and slid her palm over his still-unshaven jaw, touching him at last, and it was everything. It was hot and his jaw beneath her hand felt as perfect as it looked, and his eyes went dark and hot in an instant, even as his hand shot up to hold hers there, against his cheek.

A dare, maybe. Or a warning. But he didn't let her go.

Then there was nothing but his breath and hers, and the cloud that made in the frigid air that Michaela was aware of, yet barely felt. There was nothing but the beat of her heart and that thick, hard pulse she could see keeping pace in his throat. That searing hot, unmistakably male gleam in the dark gaze he kept locked to hers. His skin against hers again. *Perfect.* Too much and not enough.

There was nothing but the two of them. There was nothing but *this*.

So she tilted herself forward, straight up on her toes, took her life in her hands, and kissed him.

Chapter Eight

HIS LIPS WERE cold and firm against hers. And for a split second, his free hand wrapped around her upper arm, and Michaela almost thought he would set her away from him—

But then Jesse angled his head, opened his mouth, and took over.

And everything inside of Michaela exploded. Bright, white light and blistering heat. Jesse shifted, moving her back into the room without breaking the kiss, then kicked the door shut behind him. Closing them in.

She couldn't touch him enough. Her hands on that rough jaw of his, then her fingers deep in his unruly, dark blonde hair. She arched into him as he tasted her, deep and possessive, a dark, wild thrill.

He made a low noise that had no translation and yet she understood him perfectly. He shrugged his coat off, letting it drop to the floor and leaving him in the same vintage t-shirt she'd admired back in Marietta. Then his hands were on her shirt, stripping it from her, tearing his mouth from hers to pull it up and over her head. She raised her arms obediently, unable to breathe, unable to think as he peeled the long-sleeved t-shirt up the length of her arms, turned it inside out and then threw it aside.

Then he yanked her against him again as if even that long without her was too much.

This time she could feel every ridge and sculpted hollow of his perfect chest through the thin barrier of his t-shirt and the bra she still wore. And he pulled her even closer, hauling her up high against him until she wrapped her legs around his waist and her arms around his neck.

And then he took her mouth again, bossy and demanding, and she could feel it everywhere. She could feel *him* everywhere. He simply stood in the center of that dim little room with the moon pouring in from outside, held her wrapped around him, and kissed her as if he could do it forever.

He licked in deep, setting her on fire. He kissed her as if he'd been waiting for her for years. He kissed her as if this wasn't the first time, as if he'd spent decades learning exactly how to drive her wild, and he did it.

Again and again, he did it.

She could feel him, hot and hard against her molten center, and she shook as she twined herself around him. Shook and yearned and kissed him until her mouth felt swollen and her body ached and all she wanted was more.

More.

He tasted like the endless night on the other side of the door, infinite and addictive. He sank one of his strong, capable hands deep in her hair at the back of her head to hold her exactly where he wanted her. He smoothed the other hand down the length of her spine, pausing so briefly over the disruption of her bra that it took her a long moment to realize he'd unclasped it. But by then his hand had already gone lower, sliding beneath her pajama pants and her panties to grab a fistful of her bottom, not exactly gently.

But deliciously. She moaned against his mouth. She couldn't get enough.

And still Jesse kissed her like a dying man, as if this was his final act.

As if he intended to make it last.

Michaela had no idea how long he held her there, in the center of the room, kissing her and kissing her, dragging his mouth against hers and making a low noise as he did it, like some kind of approving growl. She only knew it wasn't enough and she started to tempt fate by moving her hips, in ever-so-tiny circles against him. The first time she did it, he shuddered, and his hands tightened, twin tugs of pure sensation at her scalp and at her bottom.

The second time, he groaned against her mouth and she could feel that, taste it. Like it was another lick of his clever tongue, and it was her turn to shiver out the reaction she could feel in her breasts, her core, and all her bare skin in between.

Then he was moving, staggering those last few feet to the great big bed and tipping them both flat.

He caught himself on his hands as her back hit the mattress, but he let his lower half drag hard against her, so hard it made her catch her breath and buck against him. And there was something about his weight against her, something about the sweet, slick, glorious fit of him between her legs. It was like a lit match landed in a pool of gasoline, and they both ignited.

She didn't know if she tore his shirt off or he did, if he flung her bra aside or she did. What mattered was that skin to skin contact, that unbearable perfection, her breasts pressed hard against his pectoral muscles and nothing else in the universe but this fire of theirs, arcing higher by the second.

They rolled. Their tongues tangled and tasted, punished and soothed. She was sprawled above him, dizzy with all his sheer, male perfection right there beneath her hands. They rolled again and it was Jesse on top, stretched out like a fierce predator with her breasts in his hands and their stiff points almost painful against his palms.

And still they kissed, trying this angle and that, as if there was no end. As if it was far more than lust or sex or even the sweet immolation that was wrecking Michaela from the inside out.

As if nothing between them could possibly fit into any of the things they knew, and they could taste each other forever to prove it.

She couldn't keep still. She couldn't touch him to her satisfaction, learn him well enough. She tried to trace all those fascinating ridges with her fingers, even her mouth when she found herself astride him and close at last to that sculpted abdomen of his. And she was rocking against him, the thick length of him against the seam of her sex, as if he'd be buried deep inside of her if they could only let go of each other long enough to strip off those last layers that held them apart.

It was a frenzy. It was magic. It was wild and ferocious and beautiful, too.

It was better than whole relationships Michaela had had with dim, shadowy other people whose names she couldn't remember just then. But then, she wasn't sure she could remember her own.

He flipped them again and then he held her there, his hips pinning her to the bed and his mouth at her throat. He wasn't particularly gentle, and that thrilled her too, as if it was evidence he was as wrecked by this thing as she was. He skated down her neck with his teeth, his lips, the scrape of his unshaved beard, and it made her shudder. Again and again.

Jesse moved to her collarbone, learning its length before he moved lower still, bringing his head closer to where his hands waited, and then he wrapped his fingers around one breast and plumped it up. His gaze met hers, dark and far more sinful than any chocolate she could imagine, and then he sucked the nipple deep into his hot, possessive mouth.

Michaela arched off of the bed.

He was a devil or a god, and she didn't know how to handle either one. She could only surrender. He licked and he sucked and then he moved to her other breast, as if he'd been starving for the taste of her, as if he was getting off on this as much as she was, and she didn't recognize the low moans that filled the room. The throaty gasps.

It took her a long while to understand it was her, that she was the one writhing beneath him, mindless and noisy, each tug of his hard, hot mouth sending an echoing kick deep into her core, where she melted. She melted and she shuddered and he was everywhere, his mouth at her breasts and his hard length rocking inexorably against the center of her need, and she was out of control. She was over that edge and she was falling. It was inevitable.

And he knew it.

He muttered his encouragement against her flushed skin, and everything inside of her wrenched tighter, burned hotter. She was turning inside out. She was utterly in his hands. It was bright white heat and it was rocketing straight for her, it was almost there—

And then Michaela simply exploded.

Heat and light, fire and *Jesse*.

Jesse everywhere, and he wasn't even inside her.

She shook forever, her legs wrapped around his hips and her back in a hard bow. She lost her way in too many stars. She fell and she fell and she could have kept falling. And there was nothing but the sheer exultation of all that heat for a long, long time.

Her throat felt raw and she had no idea if she'd screamed. Her hands were flung above her head as if she'd truly exploded. And Jesse was still so hard and so hot between her legs that it licked at her, a new flame when she should have been burnt out. She struggled to open her eyes, to find him in the moonlight.

His head was bent, and he was breathing hard. His arousal was pressed into her so hard it should have been painful, but then, she couldn't recall ever being quite so soft and welcoming before.

And she wanted more. She wanted him inside her. So deep she'd forget not just her name this time, but the difference between his body and hers. So deep, there would be nothing but that fire, burning higher and higher and higher.

"Jesse."

She moved her hands to slide through the raw, masculine silk of his hair, luxuriating in the heat of him, even there. His jaw was against the soft skin of her neck and she could feel the faint scrape of it with every shuddering breath she took.

And more than that, she could feel that same need, that impossible desire, in every tight muscle of that sleekly perfect body pressed so tight to hers.

"Jesse," she said again, and this time, he lifted his head.

Michaela stopped breathing. His eyes were dark, raw. Tormented. His jaw was set. He looked furious and he looked hungry and it tore through her. It tore her up.

"I can't do this," he said, with quiet ferocity. "I won't do this."

She opened her mouth, then closed it.

"I'm breaking up with him."

She wasn't sure she'd meant to say that, but it hung there between them anyway. Jesse muttered something that sounded like a curse and then he angled himself up and off of her. Michaela hated it. She mourned the loss of his body against hers like a sharp, deep grief.

He rolled to the side and sat there for a moment, his hands raked into his hair.

"Good."

Michaela wasn't certain she'd heard him correctly. She rolled to her side, trying to come to some kind of terms with the clamor inside of her, jangling nerves and molten need, want and lust and an aching thing that felt like loss.

But no shame. No guilt. Only Jesse.

"What?" she asked.

"Good," he said again, his voice as intense as the look he gave her when he turned to glare at her over his shoulder. "You should break up with him. He's a liar and a con man and a spectacular douche. But that doesn't matter. Right here, right now, you're still engaged to him."

She frowned and started to argue the point, but something in his gaze stopped her.

"Technically."

"You're either engaged or you're not, Michaela. And if

the person who thinks that he's engaged to you has no idea that you've decided to end it, I don't think it's really ended at all. Do you?" He didn't wait for her to answer, his scowl deepening. "I think a better word to describe the situation is 'cheating,' no matter what bullshit open relationship crap you've been spouting to convince yourself otherwise. That's how you felt this morning and nothing's changed since then."

She sat up then. Carefully. Aware that everything—absolutely everything—had changed, but there was no telling him that.

"I don't disagree," she said quietly. There was something moving in him, gripping him too tight, making him tense and grim. "That's what I plan to tell Terrence when I get back to Seattle."

He held her gaze for so long she thought she might break apart inside.

"Great," he gritted out. "I'm happy for you. But that doesn't make me any less of a dirt bag for cheating along with you, does it?"

JESSE DIDN'T SPEAK again until they reached Spokane, some three hours west.

It took him about that long to unclench his jaw, and to be absolutely certain he wasn't going to jerk the steering wheel over, aim the SUV for the side of Route 90, and haul Michaela back into his lap to finish what they'd started.

Because for a long time, that was the only thing he wanted. It was a physical need, like thirst. And there was nothing to do but navigate the frosty roads in the dark and wait for it to recede a little bit. Wait for that wild thing in him to settle down again so he could *think*.

He could still taste her. The temptation of her mouth. Her gorgeous breasts that had made him a praying man in an instant. Her sweet legs wrapped around him and the sounds she'd made when she came.

He was still hard—and that made him twice as furious. At her, sure, for providing the temptation. But far more at himself for succumbing to it.

They'd stared at each other for much too long in that damned room, each of them half-undressed and breathing heavily, and that hadn't helped. It had only made the wildfire that raged between them that much more apparent. Jesse had understood this woman made him into a drowning man and he had one shot to save himself. Just one.

He'd stood up, jerky and stiff, and his body had not been happy with him.

"Pack," he'd ordered.

As if she wasn't gloriously bared to her waist, magnificent in every respect. Her lips had been slightly puffy from his, her skin had been faintly pink from his stubble, and those sweet nipples of hers had still been standing up straight, like they were begging for his mouth. He knew exactly how much she wanted him. He'd felt her heat all over him, and he wasn't letting the sensation go any time soon.

She was breathing too hard, he hated that he'd made her pretty eyes go dark, and she'd swallowed as if she'd been casting around for the right words.

And he'd known if she found them, he was toast.

"Don't speak," he'd gritted at her. "I'm not kidding around here."

Her eyes had narrowed and he'd cracked a little bit, just a little bit, and too much of the hurricane he'd been trying to keep stashed down deep inside of him had rolled out. It had choked the room. Or maybe it had just choked him.

"Michaela. Please."

She'd let her head drop forward and he'd taken that as assent. Thank God. He'd slammed into the bathroom to dunk himself in ice cold water that had done absolutely nothing but piss him off, and when he'd come back out she'd dressed and had been zipping up her bag.

It had taken very little time to throw his crap together and then finally, *finally,* they were leaving that goddamned hotel room behind them.

He'd never been so happy to leave Montana, his favorite place on this earth, in his life. Not even when he'd been eighteen and thought escaping his life here was the only way he'd survive.

He snuck a glance at her now. The lazy winter sun was taking its time rising, poking tendrils of pale light through the remains of the night and over the frigid earth, spreading pink and gold in his rearview mirror. Michaela was tucked up in the seat beside him, within reach but a world away, her attention trained out the window the way it had been for hours.

Jesse almost wished she'd pretended to nap again. He was sure that would have been easier. That he'd have been less *aware* of her, somehow, instead of spending the last three hours telling himself she didn't smell like that, some haunting mix of vanilla and what had taken him two hours to decide was melon, *at him.*

"My last girlfriend's name was Angelique," he heard himself say gruffly, stamping on the gas as they cleared Spokane. He felt Michaela move beside him, could practically *hear* the sharp things she was biting back, but she didn't speak. After a moment, he continued. "Three years ago I took her home for the Christmas holidays to meet my family. I thought we were pretty serious. But by the time we headed back to Seattle after New Year's she'd moved on. With my father."

Beside him, Michaela sucked in a breath. He heard her let it out, slowly.

"Am I the Angelique in this scenario?"

He slid her a look, then returned his attention to the road.

"I can't be that guy," he told her, and he hardly recognized his own voice. The ache in it. The old, harsh wounds that he'd thought had healed but perhaps had only scarred shut. "I'm either a guy who would poach another man's woman like my father, or I'm not. And I need you to hear me when I tell you that I am *not* my father."

"I've never met your father," she pointed out, when he'd started to think she wouldn't respond. "I've only met you. If your father's in the room, I didn't invite him."

"You say that like it's easy. It's not."

"It doesn't matter what I think," she retorted, with a flare of temper that he shouldn't feel like that, like a touch. "You drew a line in the sand. Fine. I respect that. But I don't need you to sit here and lecture me on your version of morality."

"There's either right and wrong or there's chaos, Michaela," he growled. "You have to pick one."

They didn't speak again beyond the basic *do you want something to drink* and *I need a bathroom* exchanges until he rolled up in front of her building in the Belltown neighborhood of downtown Seattle. She seemed to be as frozen as he was for a moment, but then she scrambled out of her door as if she couldn't get away from him fast enough.

He hated it.

In ways he was not at all comfortable with, he hated all of it.

Jesse climbed out of the SUV and pulled her roller bag out of the far back. He wanted to insist on seeing her to her door, but he couldn't trust himself. Would he leave her there the way he knew he should? Or would he follow her in and lose himself in her the way he'd much prefer to do? How could he not know his own mind?

He set the bag down on the sidewalk and then there was nothing left to do but face each other. It was typical Seattle day, grey and damp. Michaela was bright against the muted colors of the city all around her and the threatening clouds above, and he wanted her in ways he didn't know how to catalogue, and none of this mattered anyway. It had been two days. Not even two days. The world hadn't changed.

He didn't know why it felt as if he had.

She looked at him for a long time, her hazel eyes level on his. She reached over and took the handle of her bag from him, and he let her.

"Thanks for the ride," she said, in her even, professional voice he decided he deeply loathed. He wasn't Amos Burke, known eccentric, who required careful handling. He wasn't even that loser fiancé of hers.

You aren't anything to her, a voice reminded him, and he hated that, too.

"Michaela."

"That was the most educational snowstorm I've ever been trapped in." Her lips curved, but it wasn't a smile. And it didn't go near her eyes. "It's also the only snowstorm I've ever been trapped in."

"Don't."

That curve faded away, and still she looked at him as if she could see all kinds of things in him he'd hide if he could, and Jesse would have given anything to do this differently. To be someone else. To forget about all the promises he'd made to himself and all the fury he'd carted around inside of him for the past three years.

But he couldn't do it.

She wasn't free and he wasn't that guy, and no amount of standing around on a sidewalk in downtown Seattle was going to change that. She'd betrayed her fiancé and he'd betrayed himself, and that was the only truth that mattered.

It was the only truth he could accept.

"Thank you," she said again, softer this time, and Jesse had the sense she knew exactly what was going through his head. That she could read all those twisted things in him as easily as a street sign. That she knew him inside and out, which was as silly as the rest of what had happened between them.

There was no wild fire. There was no *knowing* a stranger like that.

There were only excuses. Sex and lies and rationalizations to make sense of it all, to make people think they'd had no choice when choices were exactly what they'd had, and they'd made bad ones.

And if there was one thing Jesse refused to tolerate, it was excuses. From himself or anyone else.

He didn't say goodbye.

He walked away from Michaela like the total stranger he was to her and would remain, no matter that tightness in his chest. He climbed into the SUV and he drove away and he didn't let himself look back.

No matter how it scraped at him—no matter that it felt

like a whole lot more than a simple scrape, like it might take him to his knees if he let it—Jesse didn't look back at all.

Chapter Nine

THE DRIVE BACK to Marietta sucked.

Jesse had sorted out the problem at his job site with the usual mix of threats and promises and a few good beers, threw a different set of t-shirts and jeans into his duffel, and then headed back out toward Montana early on Thursday morning.

He told himself he was fine. *Great.* He'd been telling himself that for two days. Because why shouldn't he be great?

But there was no denying the fact he grew edgier when he hit his beloved Rockies. He was tense when he crossed the Montana state line. He moved into what could only be called a black mood when he sped past Missoula and then he found himself driving by that damned motel that didn't even appear on the map, and he didn't know what the hell he was at that point.

Lost, he thought a while later, though he knew exactly where he was. He knew these enduring mountains, this wide-open sky, as well as he knew his own hands and the things they could do. He knew the curve of the Interstate as it dipped toward Bozeman. He knew Montana like the native he was.

Geographically, he really was fine. He was a Grey and that meant he had the map of his ancestors imprinted on his body at the genetic level. His people had walked across the top of this young country, those endless forests and rolling plains, to set themselves up at the foot of a mountain that never did produce the copper they'd dreamed about. They'd settled there instead of returning to their limited prospects in Boston and they were there still. Jesse had told himself he was just carrying out the same old Grey family tradition when he'd left Billings at eighteen to set off for college with no intention whatsoever of returning, to his hometown or his father.

But the thing about most pioneers was that if things had been okay where they'd started—if they'd had decent fathers of their own, as an example—they probably would have stayed put. Jesse knew he was no exception. And then it occurred to him, as the sun was setting and he passed the turn off for Big Sky and his grandparents' place nestled there in the hills of the famous ski resort that had grown around it, that he'd let his father define every last thing he did. Why he'd left home for Seattle. Why he'd never returned, not even to a different part of Montana. Why he'd been determined to build his own company, just like Billy had, but having nothing to do with the business he knew Billy had wanted to keep in the family and would have loved to one day pass on to his son.

Hadn't Jesse chosen Angelique in part because he'd figured she was exactly the kind of woman two-bit Billy dreamed he could get, yet couldn't? It had never occurred to Jesse that Billy *could* steal his girlfriend. Had he been heartbroken all this time? Or was that just his pride, still smarting all these years later?

And all of that crap had gone down over Christmas three years back, but Billy had still ruled everything Jesse did. From how Jesse spent his holidays to how he'd handled his personal life ever since. And worst of all, to Jesse's way of thinking, Billy had invaded his head in that motel room with Michaela two days ago, too, making Jesse stop when all he'd wanted was to keep going.

Had he really thought he was betraying a sacred trust with himself by touching her?

Or had he been more worried that if he surrendered to a woman he couldn't refuse, no matter what her relationship status, he would be forced to cede the moral high ground when it came to his stance against his father?

Jesse didn't know what he hated more. That he had to ask himself the question at all—or that even when he did, he didn't know how to answer it.

Though when he kept driving, straight past Marietta and headed east toward Billings, he suspected that deep down, he had a pretty good idea about the answer, after all.

It only took another couple of hours to reach the city

he'd grown up in. Jesse turned off the Interstate and drove through his hometown with the usual sense of disbelief he'd ever lived here mixed with amazement at how little it seemed to have changed in his absence. But this time, that peculiar homecoming feeling was tempered with something else he couldn't quite define.

The city lights spread out before him as he headed toward his father's house, obscuring the practical city's more industrial aspects or at least blurring them in the dark and giving them a ghostly, desolate beauty. It was quieter than he remembered it, this late on a weekday winter's night. The refineries blew smoke against the hardscrabble city buildings, gleaming gold against the cold, while the snow-packed Rim rocks sat like solid and inevitable sentries, crowned with red-lit radio towers.

As he drove through the looming walls of snow the snowplows had left behind on their last pass, he found himself grinning slightly, and it hit him. This was home, whether he liked it or not, this pragmatic, rough-edged town that could never quite transcend its working class soul. And much as he'd spent his life pretending otherwise, he hadn't sprung into being when he'd set foot on the University of Washington campus in Seattle. He'd been raised right here, a part of this matter-of-fact place hunkered down against the big sky and the wide plains. This was where he'd learned that some beautiful things weren't necessarily obvious to the casual observer, that some things rewarded a little dedication and patience, like the sun reaching over the Rims in otherwise desolate winters. This was where he'd learned what hard work was and how not to fear the doing of it, an inbred local reality that had set him apart from his college classmates and had served him well ever since.

Fight it he had, for years now, but this was where he came from. In a very real sense, he realized then, Seattle was who he aspired to be—but Billings was who he was, down deep in his bones.

He turned that over and over in his head as he made his way along the mostly deserted streets toward his father's house. It was the same house Jesse had grown up in, though Billy had renovated it several times over the years, so it was now very much in the height of the popular nouveau ranch style. High ceilings and alder wood and a grand two story stone façade that was Billy's way of proclaiming his successes to his neighbors.

And then Jesse was sitting there in the driveway to this house he swore he'd never set foot in again, having no idea what the hell he was doing here instead of two hours west in Marietta, where he belonged. He had Michaela in his head like some kind of better angel, gazing at him with those bright hazel eyes of hers, making him wish he was the kind of man who could have claimed her when he'd had the chance. When she'd wanted him to. When he'd been stuck here instead.

Suck it up, princess, he growled at himself, and then he was out of the car and headed for the door.

The cold was a good thing. The cold felt like reason as it stung his exposed face, and he felt his tension ease down at least three degrees—to match the plummeting temperature, he imagined—as he rang the ostentatious bell his younger sister Scottie, in her usual lawyer-sharp way, had once called *Dad's mating cry*.

And then the great door swung open, and Angelique stood before him, and there was no pretending he wasn't standing here, doing this.

Jesse didn't know who was more uncomfortable in that first moment, his ex-girlfriend or him.

She was staring at him in shock, so he had more than enough time to process the fact that she wasn't quite what he'd expected. Gone was the full face of makeup, and all the mascara that had always highlighted her pale blue eyes. Gone was the darker hair dye to call more attention to the contrast between its glossy blackness and those eyes. Her hair was a rich brown pulled back into a haphazard ponytail now, and her face was scrubbed clean. She was beautiful, of course—she would always be beautiful—but this was an Angelique he'd never seen before, in cargo pants and a simple white shirt.

"Jesse," she said, as if her voice didn't quite work or she thought she might be seeing things. Then she cleared her throat. "What… What are you…?" She blinked hard, then stepped back into the house, beckoning him in. "Come in. Come in—I mean, if you want…" She looked over her shoulder helplessly, then back at him. "Your dad is here. If that's why…?"

The Angelique he'd known had never been at a loss for words. Then again, he'd made her so much the Wicked Witch of the West in his head he realized he'd half-expected her to be green and covered in warts. So maybe he didn't know her at all anymore. Not really.

"You look good," he said quietly. And she did, if different. He forced himself to say the obvious thing, because it was true and because the only reason not to say it was sheer pettiness. "Happy."

She swallowed. Hard. To her credit, she didn't look away.

"I am," she said. Then, in a rush, "Jesse, I'm so sorry that came at your expense. So very sorry. We both are."

He didn't know what to say to that. "I appreciate that."

Angelique took a breath. "If there was a way we could go back and do this in a way that didn't hurt you, we would. I want you to know that. No matter why you're here."

And he supposed he should be glad she didn't regret that it had happened, only the way it had. Because maybe it would be worse to have been betrayed like this for something that didn't matter. He opened his mouth to tell her that.

"Why *are* you here?"

That voice was as familiar to him as his own. Jesse looked past Angelique, down the length of the great foyer that was all arched wood and skylights in sheer defiance of the dizzying Montana heating bills, to see his father for the first time in over three years.

Billy stood in the doorway to the family room, flanked by two little girls in pigtails and pouts, each of them clinging to one of his legs and blinking toward Jesse with identically wide, shy eyes. The girls were adorable. Billy, meanwhile, looked exactly the same and yet older at the same time. He dressed like a man who was pushing fifty rather than sixty, in a dark Henley and that spiky dark hair of his, with a hint of a beard as an accent. Jesse supposed he was good-looking, though he hated admitting it. There was more grey in the old man's dark hair now, Jesse was pleased to note, and more lines around his eyes. And Billy stood there very straight and very defensive, a hand on each of his daughter's heads, as if he expected Jesse to start swinging at any moment.

"No fatted calf, Dad?" Jesse asked mildly. "That hurts a little."

"You want beef," Billy replied in a similar tone—or maybe not a *similar* tone, Jesse thought with some surprise, maybe it was *the same exact* tone, like he'd inherited it from Billy—"there's a new hamburger place a few miles back down the road toward town. You'll love it. It's in a hotel where, bonus, they can also put you up while you take care of your business here. Whatever that is."

"He can stay here," Angelique retorted, and rolled her eyes at Billy with, Jesse realized, the kind of absolute confidence she had never displayed when she'd been with him.

It occurred to him that all the things he'd thought were who Angelique was—the bids for his attention, the sex kitten routine—had been nothing more than insecurity. Right here, right now, she looked every inch the tough, capable Montana women he'd grown up with. That made him blink. And more, made him realize that if it was true, his split-second take on the changes in this woman, he really hadn't ever been the man for her. How could he have been?

Angelique looked back at Jesse. "Ignore him. Of course you can stay here, and for as long as you want."

"Like hell," Billy threw right back. "You're not staying under the same roof as my—"

But he didn't finish that sentence.

And it all made sense, suddenly. Jesse knew that look on his father's face. He could see the old man's fears like a scrolling marquee. Billy had stolen his very hot, much younger wife—who was the same age as his own daughters, for God's sake—from his own son. And maybe after three years and two kids, Billy figured that son might look pretty good to a woman who'd already switched allegiances once under this very same roof. Next to him, Jesse could feel Angelique vibrating slightly, with temper or emotion he couldn't quite tell, and there was a certain liberation in recognizing that whatever it was, whatever he might have figured out about what had happened between them, *this* wasn't his problem.

She wasn't his problem. His father's paranoia wasn't his problem. He didn't have to fix any of this. And yet at the same time, like it or not, these people were his family.

He wasn't sure he was ever going to truly understand his father. This was a man who had slept around so much and lied so expansively to Jesse's mother that she'd become a hermit since the divorce, preferring the company of horses on her little spread in Idaho. Billy was a salesman to his core, which meant he was a great guy to have a few beers with but was never around to clean up the mess the next day. He was a weak man and he'd been a terrible father, but then again, Jesse had built his own company from scratch exactly the way Billy had, almost as if he'd taken a few things from the old man after all. Maybe if he stopped waiting for his father to apologize, if he stopped expecting that this man, who had never changed, would do so at Jesse's command, they might discover they had a lot more in common than Jesse had ever thought.

If your father's in the room, I didn't invite him, Michaela had said.

Well, his father was in *this* room. And if Jesse didn't deal with him here, he'd spend God only knew how many more years dealing with his unresolved daddy issues in all the places Billy wasn't. And he was done with that. He wanted something better. He wanted to be free of this mess.

And if he wanted this crap behind him, he was obviously going to have to do it his own damn self.

"I'm not here to dredge up the past," Jesse said then.

Jesse recognized that tilt to his father's head, the squaring of his shoulders. He'd seen it often enough in his own goddamned mirror.

"Why show up here unannounced, if not for that?" Billy asked.

And Jesse had the same dislocating sensation he'd had driving through Billings to get here. That he might not love this place, he might define himself in opposition to it, he might have done his level best to distance himself in every way he could… but this was where he was from. This was his hometown and Billy was his father, and there was no getting around that. Billy hadn't killed anyone, or abused anyone. He and Angelique were two grown adults who hadn't even been married to other people when they'd gotten together, they had their own family now, and Jesse didn't want this anyway. He didn't want a woman who would choose his father over him, not even if the timing had been better, and he didn't want their life. Not any part of it.

He knew exactly what he wanted, and she was roughly eight hundred miles to the west and, he could only hope, disentangling herself from Terrence Polk. And he couldn't possibly deserve her if he didn't free himself of his shit the same way he'd demanded she free herself of hers.

"I heard I had a couple of little sisters," he said then, holding his father's gaze and then dropping it to look at the little girls who were still staring back at him, their eyes bright and cheeks pudgy.

He smiled at them, and waited. Slowly, very slowly, one of them smiled back.

"That's Layla," Billy muttered, his hand on her head. Then the other one smiled too, even wider. "And this is Lacey."

He heard Angelique suck in a breath beside him, as if she hadn't believed that any of this would ever happen. A quick glance showed him she was wiping tears away, covering her mouth with her hands. And when he looked back at Billy, even his father's eyes were suspiciously bright.

"It seemed like a good time to introduce myself," Jesse said gruffly. "That's why I'm here."

THAT SATURDAY NIGHT, which happened to be Valentine's Day, Michaela walked into Grey's Saloon in Marietta, Montana, on a mission.

She'd accomplished a great deal in the past few days, not least of which was paying a king's ransom or two to get the last seat on the last plane into Bozeman this afternoon. Not to mention throwing down about five times that to wrangle a suite at the gloriously restored Graff Hotel right here in town, which had, lucky for her if not for her wallet, a last minute cancellation on this most romantic of weekends. Because a woman didn't head off into the Wild West in search of a man she wasn't sure would have her and plan to bunk down in her Aunt Cathy's spare room with the twin beds.

But it was all worth it when she saw the most beautiful man she'd ever beheld, outside of a movie theater, standing at the far end of the bar, staring down at the whiskey in front of him as if he'd been doing it a while. As if he was completely alone instead of surrounded by the boisterous Saturday night crowd that heaved around him. She started toward him, not surprised that Grey's was decidedly *not* decked out in pink hearts and red garlands in celebration of the Day of Love.

She'd dressed the part herself—or anyway, she'd dressed the way she'd like to think she would have dressed had she imagined that a week ago, she'd have been meeting the man who would completely alter the course of her life. A sweet little red dress for the holiday, and for the man who didn't know she wanted to share it with him, and she'd even tried to do something with her hair. A slick of lipstick and a touch of mascara. Boots because this was Montana and it was viciously cold out there, and she wasn't going to get anywhere with Jesse if she'd tripped and broken her neck on the frigid walk over here from her hotel.

And Michaela really, really wanted to get somewhere with this man.

She knew the exact, precise moment he saw her.

Because it was like every other time their eyes had locked in those wild two days they'd spent together.

Hot. Consuming.

Epic.

He didn't move as she wound her way toward him, dodging groups of women making the typical declarations in the face of apparent singlehood, couples swaying together as if they were in private, and then the usual packs of men on the prowl and animated women looking happy enough to be prowled upon. All the usual shenanigans, and then Jesse there, like a clear, high note that cut straight through the noise.

She slipped into the space at the bar directly to his right, and then she could *feel* him. All that heat and strength. The heft of his brooding attention, his milk chocolate gaze, as he leveled it at her.

Michaela turned slowly, leaning her elbow on the bar so she could face him.

And he was exactly the way she remembered him. He hadn't been some snowstorm delusion. If anything, she'd dimmed him a bit in her head because she still couldn't believe any man could really, truly look like this.

But he did.

And he was gazing back at her as if there wasn't another woman alive, the hint of a curve on that hard mouth of his.

"Well?" she asked, after one moment dragged into a year or so, and they still only looked at each other.

"Well what?"

"Aren't you going to buy me a drink?" She lifted one shoulder, then dropped it, fully aware of what that did to the deep V neckline of her dress. And to him. "It's Valentine's Day."

"I think I can bribe the bartender into making you something hideously pink," Jesse said after a moment, dragging his gaze back to her face. "He's practically family. He can't refuse."

"Only if it's sugary and awful and will make my teeth hurt."

"You can trust me," Jesse said, and she did.

Not just about the pink drink, which was delivered with an eye roll from the dark-haired bartender who appeared only slightly less surly than the man Michaela knew to be Jesse's uncle. But she was finally here, and he was looking at her as if he could do that forever, and she figured there was all the time in the world to get into that.

"Your game is pretty dire," she told him, when the silence dragged out again. "If this is how you flirt with women, I don't think there's any wonder that you're still single."

Jesse had ordered a beer when he'd ordered her drink and he took a pull from it, then leaned closer, his smile like gold in those eyes of his.

"I don't have to flirt, Michaela. I think you know that."

"Maybe you should start."

His mouth moved into that delicious curve again, and then he reached over and stroked a finger along her shoulder. She felt that touch like a current of light, and it took her a breathless moment to realize he was doing it again, tracing the strap of this dress up and down and up again.

Making her whole body seem to liquefy and run hot, that easily.

"It wouldn't be fair," he murmured.

Jesse shifted so he was leaning against the bar too, and they were face to face again. He looked perfect. Better than perfect. He was wearing another Henley, this one a soft grey that made her hands itch to touch him, and which clung lovingly to every etched stone ridge and valley on that gorgeous torso of his.

And Michaela hadn't come all this way to stare at him, as much as she enjoyed doing exactly that.

"Technically," she said then, very distinctly, "I didn't betray anyone." His dark eyes gleamed, but he didn't say anything. "All we did was kiss." That light in his eyes turned to a very knowing, very male sort of amusement, and she felt the answering flush swamp her immediately. And everywhere. But she lifted her chin, held his gaze, and soldiered on. "It doesn't matter where."

He didn't quite laugh and that was heat in his gaze, she was sure of it, not the dark and tortured thing that had been there the last time she'd seen him.

"Believe me," he said, quiet gravel and all that fire besides. "It matters."

"I didn't break any promises," she told him, frowning at him. "It's important that you understand that, Jesse. I'm not that person." He looked as if he was going to comment on that but she forged forward. "You came out of nowhere. I'd never had the slightest interest in exploring what an open relationship meant. Maybe it always feels like cheating. I don't know. But it wasn't cheating and it doesn't matter, because I'm never going to have to worry about it again."

"Oh?" He sounded bored, but she could see that hard thing in his gaze, and she knew whatever else he was, he wasn't *bored*.

So she told him Terrence had taken a little tracking down. That she'd finally managed to find him late on Tuesday night, though she'd been reeling and exhausted from having woken up at three in the morning with Jesse in Montana, and maybe a little less composed than she should have been. She'd been waiting for Terrence outside his apartment when he'd finally turned up, and he'd looked decidedly unexcited to find her there.

"Not a great sign," Jesse pointed out now, very still against the bar, his dark eyes fixed to hers.

"Not a great greeting, either," Michaela said.

"Do we drop by on each other unannounced?" Terrence had asked, instead of saying hello. He'd smiled. Gently, the way he always had, in that way that made his lean, handsome face look much more intellectual, which she suspected he knew. "You know my feelings on dropping by. I think that speaks to a real lack of respect for emotional boundaries, don't you?"

"I'm obviously a terrible person," she'd replied, flatly. "Can we talk?"

Terrence had blinked, and then he'd ushered her inside, and Michaela had taken a minute to really ask herself if this was what she wanted to do. If she was really going to blow up her whole life after less than forty-eight hours in the company of a man she hardly knew.

"Do I have a vote?" Jesse asked darkly.

Michaela shushed him, took a sip of her sweet, pink drink, and kept going.

Terrence hadn't asked how she was or where she'd been, despite the fact it had been over a week since he'd seen her last. He hadn't mentioned all the calls he hadn't returned or the voicemails she'd left, which had made her wonder if he'd listened to them. He'd moved around his apartment in that way of his, not actually saying he'd been annoyed with her but making it clear with every single one of his gestures and the faintly clipped tone he'd used.

"So, what have you been doing all week?" she'd asked when he'd finally sat down with her, as if he'd been doing her a big favor. "You seem very busy."

And she'd let him talk. Terrence loved to talk. He'd told her about the meetings he'd had and the projects he was certain were *this close* to happening. He'd filled her in on all his many friends who'd clamored for his attention over the weekend, all of whom were people with names she was expected to recognize as movers and shakers in Seattle society, she'd been aware. And then he'd told her about last Saturday night and the blonde woman he'd noticed staring at him in this swanky hotel bar he'd been in. How he'd stared back until she'd approached him, how he'd checked in with his impulses—

"But not your voicemail messages," Michaela had interrupted him.

She'd seen something flicker in his gaze then, but he'd hidden it, sitting there on his minimalist futon in the midst of his bare white walls and pieces of modern art he'd done himself in what he called his Brooklyn phase, so languid and unconcerned. The only creatures she'd ever seen more unconcerned than Terrence were lizards, she'd thought as she watched him. Because they were, in fact, prehistoric creatures.

And next to Jesse Grey, Terrence seemed a bit more like a salamander.

"Because in this comparison," Jesse rumbled from beside her, "I'm obviously a dragon."

"Or, perhaps, a slightly more impressive gecko."

"I think we both know, Michaela, that there's nothing about me that is even remotely like a gecko."

She'd wrinkled her nose, and pushed on.

Terrence had moved closer to her. He'd taken her hands in his. And she'd let him, because she'd wanted to know. Had he snowed her completely? Or was this really who he was? And more to the point, how had she almost married him?

"Do you need a moment to take stock of your emotions?" he'd asked, solicitously. "Check in with what's happening there for you?"

"Not at all," she'd replied. "I'm one hundred percent

checked in."

"I love us," Terrence had said then, "because we can be who we are. No games. No hiding." He'd told her then, in detail, about having sex with the blonde in the bathroom of his favorite bar. In the same way he'd always told her stories like this. "Most people couldn't admit that they need that, and most women wouldn't be mature enough to know the difference between an animal attraction in a bar, fleeting and fast, and a foundation to build a future on."

"This guy is a creep," Jesse said flatly now. "Straight up. Tell me you get that."

What Michaela got was something she couldn't quite bring herself to say out loud in the press of Grey's Saloon, with Jesse so close but still not hers. Maybe he never would be hers, maybe he was nothing but a catalyst, and she told herself that was okay, too.

Because back in Terrence's apartment she'd understood something she hadn't before. That Terrence got off twice. Once in the bathroom of the hotel bar with the nameless blonde. And again there in his apartment, as he'd told her all about it. Had she never noticed that before? Had she never seen that this was the whole purpose of it for him? And maybe that was okay in a relationship where both people got off on it. If it was a thing they did together. But she'd realized in that moment that she simply hadn't cared enough either way.

Because if she'd had a man like Jesse in her life, she'd known with volcanic certainty as she'd stared at the man who adamantly *wasn't* Jesse, she wouldn't have tolerated this. She wouldn't have been able to stand the thought of him with other women. She'd have died inside if he'd shared his exploits with her at all, much less with such evident, lascivious pleasure.

Even thinking about it had made her flush with some mix of temper and emotion and need right there on Terrence's futon and she'd had no idea if she'd ever see Jesse again. She'd had no reason to worry about what he might or might not be doing, or with whom. This wasn't about him. It was about the fact that, having met him, she'd understood she *could* care more. And if she was capable of caring more, and if that level of care meant she couldn't tolerate this open door policy on a relationship, she had no business settling for this.

It wasn't fair to either of them. If Terrence really believed the things he said, if he wasn't the con man Jesse had seemed certain he was and Amos had suggested he was for years, he deserved someone who, at the very least, was as invested in this open relationship as he was. Someone who wasn't simply… numb to what he did.

But she'd wanted to know.

"I wanted to see if he was a creep," she told Jesse now, "or if he really did believe what he was saying."

"Cheating is such a silly barometer to use to determine the health of a relationship," she'd said to Terrence then, and she'd been unable to remember why she'd dated him in the first place. Amos kept her so busy and Terrence had been persistent—had that been what it was? And then she hadn't even had to sleep with him, because he'd been off having adventures, and she'd been able to smugly pretend she'd had it all while not altering her life in the least. "At the very least, it's shortsighted."

"Cheating is what immature people call things they don't have the emotional resources to work through," Terrence had said, with a self-congratulatory smile. "It's sad, really."

"I couldn't agree more," Michaela had said. "That's exactly what I told the guy I hooked up with this weekend."

Chapter Ten

JESSE'S SMILE WAS hot and dark, and made her shiver.

Michaela forgot about her drink. She forgot where they were. There was no historic saloon, no blustery winter wind rocketing down the Marietta streets outside, no state of Montana stretched out like eternity on all sides.

There was only Jesse and he was far more intoxicating.

"Tell me more about the guy you hooked up with," he said then, still smiling down at her, and Michaela felt her heart trip a bit, then start to beat harder. Deeper.

"I'm getting there," she assured him.

"I don't want to step on your moment here," he said, and she didn't see him move but he must have, because suddenly, he was like a wall around her.

Jesse reached over and slid his hand up the side of her neck and then held it there beneath her jaw, his thumb a sweet scrape from her cheekbone to her temple. Then back. It was drugging.

"But?" she asked, with what little voice she could muster when he was touching her again and she could feel *that* like an earthquake all the way through.

"Tell me if I get any of this wrong," he said in that low voice of his, and the look in his decadent eyes then was so intent, so sure, it made Michaela shake deep and long way down inside. "It felt a bit more like cheating when you did it."

"It's like you were there."

"You probably let him think we slept together, because he had that coming."

Michaela tried to look pious. "I denied it, of course. Stridently and with the full force of truth on my side."

His dark eyes gleamed. "Did he buy it?"

"As it turned out, he didn't."

"Shocker."

His hand tightened slightly, urging her closer to him, and she didn't think twice. She went, bracing her hands against that absurd chest of his that she'd tasted, now. That she knew was in fact far, far better than she'd imagined it might be when he'd been clothed.

"Do you want me to tell you the rest?" she asked, tilting her head back to look at him.

And it was the funniest thing. She could feel her feet on the sturdy floor of this old building that had weathered more than a century already. She knew she was standing still, she knew she was looking up at him, and yet she still felt as if she was falling from a great height. End over end, forever and fast.

"I got this," Jesse said. He shifted his weight slightly, but not his gaze. "I'm guessing that your man threw a fit. He probably said some stuff that if you told me, would make me think about punching him in the face. It was probably upsetting for you."

"Not as upsetting as it should have been," Michaela admitted. "That's the part that's going to haunt me, I think."

"Ghosts can only haunt you if you let them," he said gently, and there was something in his voice that made her wonder if he'd vanquished a few of his own. "But let's get back to this story we need to finish."

"Are we in a rush?"

"There's another story I want to tell," he murmured, all that light and fire in his eyes, whiskey and need. "I think you'll like it. It has a much better ending."

Michaela pulled in a breath that felt shuddery, and found she was as afraid to smile at him as she was to look away. "I broke up with him, of course. I told you I would."

"Was it painful?" Jesse's voice was dark. "Are we going to have to stand around and analyze the whole thing and talk about your feelings for one of the biggest tools in the Pacific Northwest? Because I might have a hard time maintaining a decent level of fake compassion."

"Yes, I can feel that. It's like a tsunami of empathy, sweeping me away."

"Michaela." That mouth of his was hard, his gaze intent. "I don't understand why you didn't laugh in Terrence

Polk's face when he asked you out the first time. It's inconceivable to me that you were actually planning to marry him."

"It was because of Amos," she said. Jesse blinked. "I've been asking myself the same question for days now. I'd say it was entirely Amos's fault, in fact, but I'm aware that's not fair."

It had been one of those Seattle summer nights, so warm and bright and beautiful that everyone had complete amnesia about all those months of rain. She and Amos and a few people from work had been sitting outside a bar downtown, enjoying the uncharacteristic leisure time one evening. Amos had been feeling particularly full of himself that night, breaking down his dating successes as if they were flow charts he could convert into apps to help the less fortunate—

"Like you," he'd said, and had treated Michaela to that insufferable grin of his.

And there had been no reason that should have pricked at her. No reason it should have wedged there beneath her skin. She'd played it off, knowing full well Amos would have been horrified if he'd thought his usual good-natured teasing had actually landed a blow. Then a dark-haired, intellectual-looking man at the bar had caught her eye and smiled.

"I hate that guy," Amos had said, directly in her ear as he'd texted one of the blonde twins he'd been running around with back then.

"You know him?"

"His whole type," Amos had said, shoving his phone in his jeans pocket and getting to his feet. "That whole passive aggressive, he might be a poet, he really wants you to ask him about his pain thing. Ridiculous."

"They can't all be bimbos with more silicon than brain matter, Amos," Michaela had snapped.

Amos had only grinned, and then strolled off into the summer night to further debauch himself.

But Michaela had stayed. And it turned out Terrence hadn't wanted to talk about his pain, and he didn't write any poetry—but he had wanted to take Michaela to dinner.

"Obviously, I went," she told Jesse now. "And I'll never know if I actually liked him because I liked him, or because I wanted to prove Amos was wrong. Or even because I just wanted to irritate him by dating a guy he'd written off. How sad is it that I stayed with him for all this time? I wouldn't tell you such an unflattering thing about myself, but I feel that you should know upfront what you're getting into."

Jesse grinned at her and it was a slow thing, filled with promise.

"I know," he said, "exactly what I'm getting into."

That shivered through her, but Michaela made herself go on.

"And when it was all over with Terrence," she told him, "I thought I could just go on with my life. Because nothing had changed. Terrence and I didn't live together, so there was none of that mess to deal with. Canceling the wedding was a breeze because I didn't actually have to cancel anything. I called my mother and told her I'd rethought, she said she wasn't too heartbroken by that decision, and that was it. Telling Amos the next day was harder, because he insisted on throwing an office party with cupcakes to celebrate."

"He sounds like an ass."

"God, yes," she agreed. "I told you he was like my brother. An annoying brother." She studied his beautiful face for a moment, took a breath, and then told him the rest. "And then I was sitting there on Friday morning. In my office. Everything was fine. Great, even. I had no second thoughts. I had no regrets. I had no question in my mind that I'd done the right thing." She tested her palms against his chest, marveled in the heat he pumped out like a furnace. "The only thing I didn't have was you."

Jesse grinned at her for a long time, and then he brought his other hand up, so he was holding her face between his hands.

"I was going to come back to Seattle and steal you away from him," he told her quietly. "I was going to take it slow and sweet."

"And now?"

His grin deepened, turned to pure, wicked heat.

And she felt it pound inside her like her own pulse.

"I think you better brace yourself, Michaela. We might not come up for air."

Later, Michaela would never know how they made it back into their cold weather gear and out into the street. She couldn't remember the walk from the saloon to her hotel, or even if it was as cold as it must have been. She had a vague sense of the Graff's Old West elegance as they moved through the lobby and into the old elevator, and she thought it must have taken a while to make it to her floor, but she hardly noticed.

There was nothing in the entire world but Jesse and the way he was looking at her.

She fumbled with her key in the hall outside her suite until Jesse took them from her, opening the door and ushering her inside, and then there was nothing but the two of them in another hotel room. Exactly the same as it had been a week ago, and completely, utterly different.

Too many things seemed to batter at her at once, making her worry she might trip and fall right there in the entryway—and the way Jesse looked at her when he finished locking the door, so deliciously predatory, didn't help.

She shook, outside and in. And he only smiled.

"This is a very historic hotel," she told him nervously, backing away from him, because she thought that might help her breathe. Just for a moment. Just to get her bearings. "It holds a very special place in Montana history."

His smile deepened and he came after her, stalking her into the western-style living room with all its restored Victorian splendor. She only realized she was filling him in on the amazing details of the hotel, the intricacies of the renovation that she'd read about in a brochure in the graceful desk beneath the window, when she came up against the wall outside her bedroom and stopped talking. Abruptly.

"Michaela," he said. The same way he'd said *hey* a week ago, more an order than anything else, although this time, he said it from a whole lot closer. "Breathe."

She breathed.

And realized Terrence had been absolutely right—her brain had gone to mush. But it wasn't the romance novels that had done it. They'd only paved the way.

It was all Jesse Grey.

Jesse reached over and unzipped her coat, then pulled it from her, as if he was performing a sacrament. He unwound her thick scarf from around her neck. He held out his hands and she put hers in them, then watched as he carefully eased the gloves from each one, finger by finger until she thought she might die from it. Then he stood before her for a moment, his dark gaze so hot it hurt. He took in the bright red slick of fabric she wore, wrapped around her to create a deep V at her breasts and then tight beneath them.

"I like that dress," he rumbled, and she could see the stark male approval stamped all over him and burning in that gaze of his.

"I'm glad," she whispered. "I wore it for you."

"Good," he said. His mouth crooked up in the corner.

"Now take it off."

Michaela smiled. "I will if you will."

"You've already seen me naked," he reminded her. But he shrugged out of his coat and he threw it in the general direction of the couch.

She worked on the knot of the wrap dress's tie, but Jesse was a distraction. He was stripping down in front of her, pulling off his clothes and exposing his perfect body to her view, and it would take a far stronger woman than she was to do anything but gape at him while he did it.

And soon enough he was naked and she was still staring, and he took matters into his own hands. He pulled the knot of her dress undone in two quick tugs, and then he bent a little to help her kick off her boots. She got rid of her bra herself and then Jesse hooked his fingers into her panties and tugged them down and off, and then it was done. She was as naked as he was.

For a minute, he just looked at her. And she couldn't stop staring at him.

And she thought maybe neither one of them could believe this was really happening.

But then Jesse made a very low, very male noise. He reached over and pulled her into his arms, sweeping her up like some kind of romantic heroine to hold her against the wall of his chest. She tipped her head back and met that gaze of his, so dark, so rich. So focused on her it made her tremble. And burst into a wet, hot heat.

He still didn't kiss her. She could feel his heart like

thunder in his chest, and maybe that was why she could breathe again. And smile at him as he took her through the door and into the bedroom.

She still had so many things to say to him, but it felt sacred in her room, hushed and reverent. It was an elegant sweep of a room, from the high four poster bed to the paneled wardrobe on the far wall, and Jesse laid her down in the middle of the mattress and then climbed up beside her, stretching out the sculpted heat of his perfect body along the length of her side.

Just the way she'd dreamed he had back in that motel room, when she'd been wearing all those layers, and he'd done nothing more than touch her tank top strap.

It seemed like a lifetime ago.

"So I was right," Michaela said, not sure if she was smiling at him or if it was simply that she felt like some kind of beacon, burning too hot and too bright from within, making them both shine. "You only make sweet, soulful, tender love after all."

Jesse grinned in a way that was entirely too male to be sweet, and then he reached over and wrapped his hand around her neck, tugging her to him.

"Not quite," he said, and then he set his mouth to hers and all hell broke loose.

SHE TASTED LIKE light. She tasted like sex and sugar and he was a goner.

Jesse knew if he'd dared kiss her like this—or at all—while they'd still been out there in Grey's, his uncle would have doused them with a pitcher of water. Or called the fire department.

Even here, stretched out on a bed with a locked door behind them and all the privacy in the world, it was almost too much.

Her mouth was carnal perfection, made to drive him wild with need and wonder, and he couldn't get enough. He didn't think he ever would.

They rolled on the bed, kissing each other as if their lives depended on it. Hands sank in hair. Fingers dug into each other's backs, sides, butts. Michaela on top, a feast and a joy, writhing against him. Michaela beneath him, cradling him, holding him in the place he most wanted to stay and then slowly driving him to the point of insanity with each little rock of her hips. And his world.

And this time, she was his. This time, he wasn't going to stop.

This time, there was no one in the room but the two of them.

He rose above her then, moving from her lush mouth to take stock of her, fully naked beneath him. At last. He treated her sweet neck like a prayer, her perfect breasts like a blessing, and then he lost himself for a while in the thrust of her tight nipples, the hollow between her breasts, the warm shadow beneath each one.

When she was moaning beneath him, he moved on,

trailing fire and longing over that belly of hers he'd first felt with his ice cold palm. Today there was nothing the least bit cold about him, or her, and he exulted in that. The wild heat. The exquisite fire. The shallow indentation of her navel and then beneath, where she was molten hot and ready for him.

He kissed her at the top of one thigh, then moved closer to the heart of her need, moving near that turgid center but never quite making it. Again and again, until she made a sound of sheer, feminine frustration that made him grin.

"You're torturing me!" she accused him, with a fist in his hair as punctuation.

"This is as good a time as any to go over a few ground rules, I think," he told her, and it was a fight to keep his voice that lazy, as if none of this was affecting him.

She called him a name and he laughed.

"What rules?" Michaela demanded, and she was the most beautiful thing he'd ever seen, splayed out there before him, her hazel eyes wild and half-gold with desire, her cheeks flushed red. Her dark hair was a tangle around her and she was trembling still, her lovely thighs and those magnificent breasts too lovely to bear, and she was perfect.

Utterly perfect.

"I don't believe in open relationships," Jesse told her, very seriously. "I believe in hard boundaries and kept promises. I believe in so many ties to each other you can't breathe, and then a few more. I believe in deep, dark, messy, irrational love that lasts forever, works itself out in bed, and never, ever invites anybody else to the party. Or I don't see the point."

He saw the way she flushed, the way the awareness in her gaze turned to something else. Something he recognized. Something it was too soon to say out loud, too soon to think. But he knew she could see the same thing all over his face, and who cared if it had only been a week.

She caught her bottom lip between her teeth as if she was thinking it over, when he could see she was hiding a smile. "That sounds very immature."

"It is," he agreed. "It definitely is."

And he tasted her then, because he could. He licked his way through her heat, humming at the way she bucked and the sharp, high gasp she let out. And then he looked up at her again, and could feel the edginess in his own smile.

"No sharing," he said. "And let's be clear, Michaela. When the time comes, I'm not getting married in a courthouse. It's not going to be about taxes. I want you in a dress like a cake, neck deep in flowers, and a cattle brand or a big ass ring, your choice, to make sure there's no doubt about your status. Wedding comas and a football team of bridesmaids. I want to make it so hard for you to walk away from me you come to me on your knees if you have to."

"Be still my beating heart," she whispered, her voice a broken thing, as her hips moved restlessly beneath him. "And what do I get if I subject myself to this conservative, conventional nightmare?"

He grinned, watching her catch her breath at that, feeling her shiver and yearn where he held her beneath him.

"Me," he said gruffly. "You get me."

"That sounds like an excellent trade," she whispered.

And Jesse bent his head and took her in his mouth.

She didn't speak a coherent word for some time. First he sucked the hard little center of her need deep into his mouth, riding her out as she shattered around him, crying out her pleasure to the elegant old walls around them. Then he started all over again, learning every inch of her sweet folds, taking his time, tasting her as he built the fire anew.

When she was moaning out his name again, right there on the edge, he pulled away and made his way up the length of her body, tasting her excitement as he went.

And then, at last, he settled himself between her legs, nudging up against her delicious softness.

Michaela wrapped her arms around his neck and she draped her legs over his hips, and time stopped for a while as they paused there for a breath, stretched out together on the edge of everything he'd ever wanted. And then he pushed in gently, testing the fit of her and the slick, addictive heat, before he thrust in deep.

They both groaned.

And then the fire took over.

Jesse tried to set a slow pace, but she fit him too well. She arched into him, meeting each thrust, rocking against him and making him feel wild and out of control. She dug her nails into his back and pressed her open mouth to his neck, and then sobbed out words he couldn't begin to understand against his throat.

He reached down between them and found her sweet center, then pressed down hard, and felt her go stiff beneath him. Then break apart into heat and light and this time, as he threw her off the side of the planet, he went with her.

Later, much later, after getting sidetracked in the shower and then again on the thick carpet at the foot of the stately bed, Jesse stretched out in the bed with Michaela tucked up against him. She rested her chin on his chest and smiled at him.

"That's a pretty good start," she said.

He felt his mouth crook and understood this woman was going to keep him smiling, whether he liked it or not.

He liked it. He more than liked it.

"Start?" he asked, in mock outrage. "That was more than a *start*. You're in deep, Michaela. Better start swimming."

Her hazel eyes heated up, and he didn't think she had any problem with that. And this was too new, he knew, to say the things he could feel simmering in the air between them. But he had no doubt that was where they were headed. He could see a whole future in her eyes. He could taste it on her skin.

He ran a hand up her lovely back and enjoyed the way she shivered. They'd spent two days in a snowstorm facing their pasts and finding their future, and maybe that expedited things. Maybe that was why he felt as if he'd always known her. Why he knew he always would.

Why he knew exactly what this was, no matter what words he used or didn't.

Yet.

"I know how to swim," she told him. "Don't worry about me. But you have an obligation to fulfill."

He didn't try to hide his entirely too satisfied smile, then.

"Are you sure? I thought I told you about the dangers of faking, Michaela. I can tell. I can also tell when you're not faking, which by my count comes to—"

She smacked him on the chest. "Idiot. That's not what I meant."

He felt his heart in his chest, ten sizes too big. He thought of those little girls who were his sisters now, whom he might have continued to ignore were it not for this woman and the impetus she'd given him to face off with his past at last. He thought of the work they each did and how easy it had been to slip into work mode that snow day in the motel. How lucky he was to have found someone who could understand, at last, that kind of focus and drive—and who had her own, in spades.

He thought about all the thousands of ways this woman had been made for him, how she fit him, and he tightened his arms around her and rolled them over, coming up above her and letting her cradle him again.

It was never going to be enough. He was never going to get enough of this woman.

"I told you in the saloon," he said, gazing down at her. "This story is going to have a very happy ending."

And Michaela smiled up at him, her bright eyes alight and her arms around his neck.

"I'm sure it will," she told him. "I've never been more sure of anything in my life. But first—" and she let her smile widen, let it take over the world "—you owe me that date."

The End

If you enjoyed these Bachelor Auction stories, you will love the rest of the Bachelor Auction series!

Bound to the Bachelor

Sarah Mayberry

Bachelor at Her Bidding

Kate Hardy

The Bachelor's Baby

Dani Collins

What a Bachelor Needs

Kelly Hunter

In Bed with the Bachelor

Megan Crane

One Night with Her Bachelor

Kat Latham

Buy now from your favorite online retailer!

About the Author

USA Today bestselling author **Megan Crane** writes women's fiction, chick lit, work-for-hire YA, and a lot of Harlequin Presents as Caitlin Crews. She also teaches creative writing classes both online at mediabistro.com and at UCLA Extension's prestigious Writers' Program, where she finally utilizes the MA and PhD in English Literature she received from the University of York in York, England. She currently lives in California, with her animator/comic-book artist husband and their menagerie of ridiculous animals.

Visit her website at megancrane.com or caitlincrews.com.

Thank you for reading

In Bed with the Bachelor

If you enjoyed this book, you can find more from all our great authors at TulePublishing.com, or from your favorite online retailer.

Made in United States
Troutdale, OR
11/01/2024

24345643R00118